Hot Chocolate

Also by David Brelsford and published by Ginninderra Press

Crossroads

Bernie

David Brelsford

Hot Chocolate

All royalties from the sale of this book will be donated to the Motor
Neurone Disease Association of Tasmania.

See page 120 for information about motor neurone disease.

Hot Chocolate
ISBN 978 1 76109 087 5
Copyright © David Brelsford 2021
Cover image: Luisa Peter on Unsplash

First published 2021 by
GINNINDERRA PRESS
PO Box 3461 Port Adelaide 5015
www.ginninderrapress.com.au

Contents

All Hail the Jerusalem Artichoke

'Mutton dressed up as lamb,' said George as we sat down to a communal breakfast. 'The old man's gone gaga.'

'How old is she?' I asked.

'Forty-four, forty-six, something like that. Trying to look thirty-two. It's disgusting.'

'If Mum was alive today, she'd be turning in her grave,' I said.

'Well, good luck to him, say I.' This was Leila.

'Are you stupid?' I said. 'If he marries her, we lose our inheritance. Dad's got a bit put aside. One third will do us each very nicely.'

'Oh,' she said.

Yeah, Oh.

'We've got to stop him. I've got nothing against him having a fling,' said George, who's been married three times already, 'but this floozy will get it all when he karks it if they get married.'

'How old's Dad again?'

'Seventy-two. You'd think he'd know better.'

'No fool like an old fool,' said Leila, who is the oldest of us all and, I've always thought, is a bit of a dill.

'What are we going to do?'

'Well, Dad's invited us all to meet her. Next Saturday at Johnny Pinito's Restaurant.'

'I know it,' said Leila. 'Bit of a sleazy joint.'

'It'll fit right in,' said George. 'I tell you, we've got problems.'

I should explain that Dad sold his house about two years ago – got a good price for it – and invested the money so that George, Leila and me get one-third each when he dies. Until then, he stays with each one of us for four months of the year. It's no real problem, he's been no trouble – until this floozy appeared and turned his head.

Well, we went to this restaurant to meet her, Fiona was her name, and it was immediately obvious that George's observation had been correct.

A stomach that wanted to sag but was held in by a corset. Breasts that wanted to sag but were held up by some wonderbra. A chin that would double soon, you could see. Make-up was good, I'll give her that, but I reckon she'd had a lot of practice. I don't know if she had varicose veins under those stockings but I wouldn't be surprised. And haemorrhoids? Well, I don't know, I don't know.

Of course we were all politeness and smiles. Dad was obviously besotted, couldn't keep his eyes off her. We sat outside on a warm evening and after our meal I got out a fag.

'Cigarette?' I offered.

'No thanks, I don't smoke,' she replied with a tightening of her upper lip.

Oh, you self-righteous bitch, I thought, and a couple of medieval tortures came to mind.

It was a strained evening and even George couldn't make any silly jokes. We said our goodnights and the three of us quietly arranged to go back to my place straight away.

'She's got him by the throat,' said Leila. Only she didn't say throat, but I'm trying to keep things a bit clean around here.

'If he marries her, he'll be dead inside six months,' I said.

'What a way to go!' said George.

'Stop it!' I said. 'This is bloody serious. She'll get it all and we won't be left with the skin of a fart.'

'The skin of a fart!' laughed George. 'That's a good one.'

No wonder his first two wives left him.

'Hey, that's given me an idea!' said Leila.

'Oh yeah?'

'Yous ever heard of Jerusalem artichokes?' she said.

'Eh?'

'Jerusalem artichokes.'

'What about them?'

'They make you fart. There's some chemical in them that gives you flatulence.'

'Gives you what?' I said.

'It's a fancy word for farting,' said Leila, looking at me out of the corner of her eyes. Ooh, she can be a madam sometimes.

'So?'

'Don't you see?' she said. 'If we feed him Jerusalem artichokes, he'll be farting all the time. It'll put her off, the fastidious bitch. We might come out of this smelling like roses after all.'

'Smelling like Rose's what?' sniggered George.

I reckon it won't be long before wife number three figures she's had enough.

'Well, he's staying with George at the moment,' I said. 'So that won't work. I can't see Heidi doing that.'

Heidi is George's current wife. She's Swedish and she's been married to him for about a year, and from what I've seen of her, she's only good for one thing and it ain't cooking, although it rhymes.

'That's okay,' said Leila. 'I'll fix up some food and take it round for them to give to him. That okay with you, Georgie?'

She calls him Georgie and he hates it, which is why she does it. But George couldn't refuse, of course. Not with so much at stake.

Leila's a good cook, I will say that, and it shows. Her hubby's as fat as a pork pig. Me, I'm adequate I guess, but I'm lucky. My old man will eat anything. I swear if you gave him a raw rat with a couple of olives he'd scoff it down.

'He's due to come to you anyway in a couple of weeks, Leila,' said George.

'Bewdy,' she said. 'I'll fix him. I'll give him Jerusalem artichokes for breakfast, dinner and tea.'

'Won't he get tired of them?'

'Not the way I'll do them. He won't know he's eating them half the time. And he likes a bit of curry too. Can you imagine what that'll produce?' And she lifted her eyes skywards.

'You sure this is all gonna work?' asked George.

'You got any better suggestions?'

'I'll fix that friggin' flouncin' floozy,' said Leila.

Only she didn't say friggin', if you get my drift. She can be crude at times, can our Leila.

But she got to work and took around various dishes laced with these artichoke things. Heidi didn't mind. It saved her cooking all the time, which she hates anyway, and all they had to do was keep it quiet from Dad. That was easy, he was either out playing golf or cavorting with his fancy lady, so Leila had plenty of opportunity to slip the food into George's place without Dad knowing.

And when, two weeks later, Dad moved into Leila's, she really got cracking. Jerusalem artichokes in just about every meal, sometimes mashed or boiled or roasted, or even powdered and mixed in with the gravy, or the custard, or even his coffee. And because Dad likes a bit of curry with his meals, it tended to mask the taste all the time.

And the flatulence part was working too. Leila reported that the air turned green sometimes and we reckoned it wouldn't be long before that fastidious floozy Fiona started getting sick of it.

Well, we thought we saw it coming when Dad asked me and George round to Leila's place one night, and he looked serious before we even started.

'Me and Fiona aren't going to get together, not in the normal way,' he said.

Hallelujah!

'Why not, Dad?'

'Fiona's got a condition,' he said. 'She told me the name of it but I can't remember. Some long scientific name, amy-something-or-other. Anyway, what it means is that she's gradually losing her faculties and the doctors reckon she's only got about two years to live.'

'Oh, Dad!' I said with genuine concern.

'Yeah, well, what it means is that she has to go for treatment every day and she can't take too much stress. We've agreed that I'll just visit her one night a week for a few hours, for…well, you know…'

'For conjugal visits,' said George, as insensitive as ever.

'Yeah. Well we won't be getting married or anything like that. Fiona's hearing is starting to go, she's going to have to get strong glasses soon, and she's lost her sense of smell already.'

Lost her sense of smell?

'Well, there it is,' he said. 'I'm seventy-two, so I won't be around too much longer. I guess we'll be a comfort to each other in our final years.'

We sat stunned. But then he perked up a bit.

'I must say, though, I'm enjoying my stay with you, Leila. What's that food we're eating a lot of?'

'Jerusalem artichokes,' said her hubby. The bloody fool, couldn't he keep his fat mouth shut?

'Well, I love them,' said the old man. 'Keep them coming! I can't get enough of them.'

And that's how it's all panned out. Fiona turned out to be not such a bad sort after all. We've visited her a couple of times and she's more down to earth than we first thought.

Only trouble, of course, is that Dad's still farting. And the Jerusalem artichokes are his favourite food. He even asks for them in restaurants and wants to know how to grow them in the garden.

'It's backfired on us a bit,' I said.

'Backfired!' snorted George. 'That's a good one.'

We ignored him.

'It's the price we have to pay,' said Leila. 'For trying fix up Fiona the flouncing floozy, we each have to suffer four months of father's friggin' farting.'

Only she didn't say friggin'.

Amount Owing

'There's Bruce again,' I said. 'I think he spends his whole day just walking around town.'

'Yes,' said Freddie.

'I only found out recently that he's John's brother. You wouldn't think so, would you? John seems to have got all the brains in that family.'

Freddie smiled in agreement. John was a justice of the peace, played the double bass in the local small orchestra, had been a respected boxer, and was the secretary of the local community association. He had the look of a fit and healthy man, sharp of intellect and quick of movement.

Bruce, on the other hand, had a pot belly and walked slowly with his hands in his pockets. He would say 'truce' instead of 'truth', or 'sgetti' instead of 'spaghetti.' Even though we saw him often when we went into town, you couldn't say he was one of the town's 'characters'. He was too insipid for that. He walked the streets all day, so it seemed, always in his shirt sleeves even on the coldest day. And as far as I know, he never drank or smoked.

I had done some work with John, volunteering on a community project. A group of us – myself, John, Freddie and a couple of others – would meet at the weekends and head out into the bush to eradicate invasive weeds.

'Does he live in town?' I asked by way of conversation.

'Yes,' said Freddie. 'Just up George Street.'

I didn't want to appear too nosy, and anyway it was none of my business, but when I was working on the weed cutting, I brought it up with Freddie again while we were out of John's hearing.

'He gets some sort of pension,' I was told.

'He doesn't seem mentally disabled,' I said.

Freddie shrugged. 'Dunno, mate. He's capable of looking after himself but John always makes sure he's okay.'

'He lives alone, then?'

'Yep.'

And that was the end of the conversation. Or so I thought. But later that day when I was alone with Freddie, he suddenly said ,'Ol' Bruce was a good boxer, you know. Better than John.'

'Ah!' I said. I thought I saw some pattern here. 'But he got knocked about too much, eh? And that's left him like he is?'

Freddie pursed his lips. 'I don't know. Maybe.'

I must say I enjoyed conversing with John. Without being academic, he seemed knowledgeable on a range of subjects. He had obviously experienced a lot of life – unlike his brother who it seemed had never left the precincts of the town. We became quite friendly. One day I was gratified when he asked me if I could help him on a little job – nothing to do with our volunteer work.

'Sure,' I said. 'What is it?'

'Bruce needs to have his lounge room painted. He can't do it all himself. Do you think you could help us one afternoon?'

So the following Saturday saw me at Bruce's house ready to paint. It was a modest little cottage tucked away in a quiet part of town. The garden seemed well kept and there was not a thing extraordinary about the place.

The three of us, Bruce, John and myself, set to work. John was the natural leader. It was my job to do what I was told and Bruce naturally fell into that mould too. Furniture was pushed out of place so that we could paint the walls, and a couple of photographs had fallen over on top of a cabinet.

We worked steadily and by lunchtime had done most of it.

'We'll be finished by mid-afternoon,' said John.

After lunch, while Bruce was occupied washing the dishes, I thought

I would bring up the subject again with John. 'Freddie tells me that Bruce was a good boxer,' I said.

John nodded. 'He sure was. Could've been state champion if he'd wanted to be.'

'Why didn't he?'

A defensive look came over John's face. 'He retired too early.'

Well, that begged the question 'Why?' but I didn't get the chance to ask it because Bruce returned and we resumed work.

After we finished the painting, it was time to put the furniture back and I re-erected the two photographs that had fallen over. My brow furrowed and I looked more closely at one of them. But both John and Bruce were nearby and I kept quiet for a time.

I waited for the right moment and when Bruce was out of sight I said to John, 'Who's the girl in that photograph?'

John didn't hesitate. 'Madeleine,' he said. 'Madeleine Fry.'

'Yes,' I said, and John looked at me curiously.

But Bruce was back again and I knew this was not the time.

When we had finished and had said goodbye to Bruce and were walking out to our separate cars, John said to me, 'Do you know this Madeleine girl, then?'

'Knew,' I said. 'Past tense. I knew her. In Cessnock, where I come from.'

'How did you know her?'

This was tricky ground, after I'd seen the photo with Bruce and Madeleine.

'I was her boyfriend for a while,' I confessed. 'About four years ago, before I came here.'

'And did she ever mention this town?'

'Yes, she did, now I come to think of it. She said she used to live here. But we broke up before I decided to come here.'

'You broke up?' he prompted.

'We were only together for a couple of months. She'd just arrived in Cessnock and we got together quickly. Then she told me she was pregnant. Well, I wasn't the father, the dates were all wrong. So we parted. I've always felt a bit guilty about that.'

John was looking straight at me. 'And now,' he said, 'Now that you've seen that photo of Bruce and Madeleine, who do you think the father was?'

My jaw dropped. 'Oh hell!' I said. 'Bruce was the father of Madeleine's child?'

'Yes,' said John. Then he touched my arm. 'Was it born okay?'

'Yes,' I said. 'A boy. That's all I know.'

I looked up at the clouds and the blue sky and a wistful sadness came over me. 'She was a nice girl,' I said.

'She was a lovely girl,' said John.

'Why did she leave Bruce?'

We were sitting on a seat now, some distance from Bruce's house.

'She didn't like his boxing,' said John. 'He was a good boxer, better than I ever was. He got a chance at a shot for the state title and he trained hard for it. She resented it all: said she didn't want to be married to a bruiser. Bruce wasn't a bruiser, he was a very scientific boxer. But she didn't understand that. It got to the point where she said it was either her or his boxing. He tried to explain to her that he was committed now, it was only a week away, he couldn't back down now. But she left him. That hit him harder than any uppercut. When he went in to the big match, his heart wasn't in it. And he got belted. That's why he is as he is.'

'He's a decent harmless man,' I said.

'And heartbroken,' said John. 'He's never got over it.'

'Does he know that she had his baby?'

'No.' He grabbed my arm. 'And for God's sake, don't tell him!'

But I knew what I must do. I still had a sister in Cessnock and that was a good excuse for me to return for a visit. But of course that wasn't the real reason.

Cessnock is a pleasant town and I have often regretted leaving. But a man must go where the jobs are, and anyway I had wanted to see a bit more of the world.

It didn't seem to have changed much in the four years I had been away. The trees had grown a bit taller, some had been chopped down for road widening, but overall it was the same friendly place I had grown up in. My sister and her husband accommodated me but I didn't tell them why I was really there.

Facebook, White Pages, and general enquiries amongst old acquaintances soon revealed where Madeleine Fry was living.

I hesitated before visiting. What if she was married now? Would she be pleased to see me – the man who had given her the flick once he'd learnt that she was pregnant with someone else's baby? And most important of all, would she agree to my proposition?

Well, there was only one way to find out. I took a deep breath and knocked on the door.

And there she was! As lovely as ever! She still had that serene look and that shortish blonde hair that I had always found so attractive.

She recognised me straightaway. 'Alan!' she said.

I nodded as a toddler came up and held the hem of her skirt.

She looked down at him and smiled. 'This is Timothy,' she said.

In her lounge room, I stroked her pet Labrador as she made cups of coffee. It was obvious there wasn't a man around: no pictures of ardent young suitors, no magazines or signs of any sort that said 'man'.

'There's just me and Timothy,' she said. 'And Rocky, of course.'

'Rocky?'

'The dog,' she smiled. 'I named him after Rocky Marciano. He was a famous boxer, you know.'

'How come you didn't get a boxer dog?' I said, somewhat foolishly.

Oh, and the look that came over her face!

'No, I couldn't do that!'

I leaned forward. It was time to be bold. I even reached out to touch her hand, and let it rest there. 'Madeleine, there's a man who's breaking his heart for you. He's wasting his life away because you separated. He's like an empty shell. There's only one girl for him, and that's you. And you know who I'm talking about. He's the father of your boy.'

And as I spoke the tears poured down her cheeks.

'I can't,' she said. 'I can't.'

'Why not?'

She shook her head. 'We quarrelled. I can never forget that.'

'Do you know what happened in that boxing match?'

Her eyes were wide. 'No.'

'He got beaten. Well and truly. Thrashed. I know his brother and he told me that Bruce's heart wasn't in it.'

'Oh God!' she said, and covered her face. 'Oh God!'

'Come and visit him, at least,' I said. 'Come and see him. Let him see his son. You owe him that much.'

She was breathing heavily and still crying. It was time for one last effort.

'Madeleine,' I said. 'That man needs you. You're the only one who can heal him. He's a good, kind, gentle man. But he needs you. And, I think,' leaning back and taking my hand from hers, 'I think you need him too.'

'Why are you crying, Mummy?' said little Timothy as he came to her.

Rocky the dog touched his wet nose on her knee.

She was crying but she was nodding vigorously now. 'Yes,' she said. 'Yes.'

She looked at her boy and managed a smile, even through all those tears. 'We might go on a little trip, Tim,' she said. 'To meet a friend.' Then she looked at me. 'I don't have a car,' she said. 'Do you think we could come with you?'

Well, of course! It was a pleasurable experience to be in her company again for a few hours, even though we didn't converse a great deal and she slept some of the time.

'How are we going to approach this?' I said as we drove into town. It was evening and a frost was already threatening.

'I'll stay at a hotel overnight,' she said, 'And see him tomorrow morning. That will give me time to think what I'm going to say.'

But when we got to Bruce's cottage next morning, he wasn't there.

'He's probably walking around town somewhere,' I said. 'He does that a lot.'

I knew where to find John, his brother, but when we met up with him, we saw immediately that something was wrong.

'Bruce had a brain haemorrhage yesterday,' he said. 'He's in intensive care at the hospital.'

Madeleine looked at me with panic in her eyes and I took the cue immediately. 'Let's get over there!' I said.

The medical staff wouldn't let us see him straightaway. 'Only family members are allowed,' they said.

'I'm the mother of his child,' said Madeleine. 'I was his de facto wife.'

I had to smile then at her assertiveness. And the hospital staff understood.

'Be very careful,' they said as she was ushered in. 'He's very sick.'

I sat outside and waited. She was with him for a long time. A staff member entered a couple of times to see if everything was all right, and once, through the quickly opened door, I caught a glimpse of Madeleine sitting by his bedside, holding his hand, talking to him, with little Timothy looking on. Then the door closed and I saw no more.

After a full two hours, the staff came and told her she must go now. They were very understanding and courteous, but insisted that he need his rest.

I drove her back to her hotel and she didn't say a word. She was obviously deep in her own thoughts.

When we got there, she just said, 'Thank you,' and we agreed to go again later that evening.

I went to see John and asked him what had happened. 'He collapsed yesterday morning. Good job I was with him at the time. If he'd been out on the streets, he could have died.'

'Yesterday morning?' I said. 'What time?'

'Pretty late. Just before lunchtime.'

I said nothing but breathed heavily and turned away. That was just the time I had been persuading Madeleine to come and visit him!

'There's nothing we can do now,' said John. 'It's in the lap of the gods.'

'I don't know about gods or God,' I said, 'But Madeleine's his guardian angel.'

John smiled. 'She's a lovely girl, isn't she?'

'Angelic!' I said, and meant it.

That evening, I drove her to the hospital again. And again she sat with him, holding his hand and talking to him. He lay with his eyes closed and there was no way of knowing if he could hear her. She told me all this when she came out; I had been looking after Timothy after they said again that I couldn't go in.

It was good to feel that she was confiding in me and I hoped that I was providing some sort of comfort for her.

But the next morning brought the worst news of all. When we went in, the hospital staff called us both aside and very quietly informed us that Bruce had died overnight.

She wept on my shoulder then. And even though I grieved with her for the death of her former love, I felt a certain hope that perhaps she would now be mine.

I drove her back to her hotel and left her to sleep, saying we would meet tomorrow. Then I went back to meet John.

'I want to pay for the funeral,' I said.

He looked at me in surprise. 'Why?'

I couldn't explain it to him fully. I just felt under an obligation, somehow. Maybe it was because I had parted with Madeleine when I discovered she was pregnant. I don't know.

'I'm his brother,' said John. 'We'll pay for it between us.' And I nodded in agreement.

But when I went to meet Madeleine the following morning, ready to drive her back to Cessnock, I got a shock.

'She's gone, sir,' said the hotel clerk. 'Checked out early this morning.'

'Did she say where she was going?'

'No, sir. Sorry.'

Well, she had no car and she was almost certainly going back to Cessnock, but a check at the train station got me nowhere. The train had long gone by then, anyway.

At least I knew where she lived in Cessnock. I figured she was grieving and wanted to be left alone, so it was two weeks before I was once again entering my native town. And when I got to her address, I got another shock.

She was gone!

'Where?' I asked a neighbour.

She was a fat woman, chewing a slice of bread with her mouth open. 'Dunno, mate,' she said between belches. 'She just went. I never spoke to 'er much, 'er an' that kid.'

Further investigations all fell flat. No forwarding addresses, no farewells to anyone, nothing.

What could I do?

Notices in papers, enquiries amongst old friends, all led nowhere. Madeleine, the girl who could have made me happy, had disappeared from my life.

Bruce was buried and John and I paid the funeral costs between us.

We tended to drift apart after that. I gave up going to the volunteer group, and if I saw John around town, we would chat cordially for a few minutes before moving on.

I haven't made much of myself. I have a steady job and I've never got into trouble. I don't smoke or take drugs, and it's been many years since I got drunk. Thirteen, to be exact. Because when I finally realised that Madeleine was lost to me, I hit the vodka bottle for one horrendous weekend, and then told myself, through my vomit, that I would never love another woman.

And I haven't formed any lasting relationships since then. Oh, I've had the occasional girlfriend over the years, but none of them moved me in the way I knew Madeleine could have.

Thirteen years, and I am growing older. In my spare time, I took to wandering the streets, nodding and smiling at old acquaintances, no particular destination in mind, just wandering, drifting. And the irony of it was not lost on me, oh no. I knew that's what Bruce used to do because he had lost the love of his life, and I knew I was doing the same thing. And somehow, strangely, that gave me a sense of comfort.

Then one day I saw John in the street, and as usual we stopped for a chat.

After we had exchanged pleasantries about the weather and the dreadful state of politics – all the usual things – John said, 'I had a Facebook message from Timothy Fry the other day.'

Timothy Fry! That was Madeleine's son! He'd be seventeen now.

My heart jumped.

'What did he say?' I asked as casually as I could.

'He was enquiring about Bruce, his father. Wanted dates of birth and death, I think for some documents he needed.'

I interrupted him before he said any more. 'I'll look him up on Facebook,' I said. 'See ya!'

And I hurried home. For the first time in many years I felt as though I had a purpose.

And there he was! Yes, that was him! Timothy Fry, just seventeen, just left high school, son of Madeleine Fry. That's all it said.

I messaged him straight away.

'I was an old friend of your mother,' I wrote. 'I'd like to meet you.'

And of course I didn't add that I was much more interested in meeting his mother again, even after all these years. I knew she would be just as beautiful as ever.

'I live in Canberra,' he wrote.

'I'll be there!' I replied.

I raced up to Canberra. My eyes were shining, I'm sure of it, and a smile was not far from my lips. I was going to meet up with Madeleine again! I wondered what we would say to each other. But maybe she had a man now – and my heart chilled. But not for long. I told myself not to be stupid.

Timothy Fry, a good-looking young man of seventeen, greeted me and ushered me inside. This was the big moment: I was going to meet Madeleine again!

'Where's your mother?' I said.

He looked at me in surprise. 'Mum's dead,' he said. 'I thought you knew.'

'Madeleine is dead?'

'Yes.'

'How long ago?'

'Six months.'

'How did she die?'

'She had motor neurone disease. She'd had it for years. She was pretty helpless over the last couple of years. It was a blessing in the end.'

I sat down and put my head in my hands. I should have known, of course. Instead of contacting John, Timothy would have been able to get his father's details from Madeleine if she had been alive.

'If only I'd known,' I said. 'I could have helped her.'

'Are you the other man?' he asked suddenly.

'Other man?'

'She told me about my father. But she sometimes spoke of another man who she knew and had been keen on her.'

'Yes, that was me. Do you remember coming with your mother to see your father when he died? You were four.'

'Only very vaguely,' he said.

'While your mother was spending time with your father, I was look-ing after you in the hospital. Do you remember that?'

He smiled apologetically. 'I'm sorry,' he said. 'I really can't say I do.'

That was only natural. Not many of us can remember details like that from our very early years.

'Why didn't your mother contact me? She knew where I lived.'

'She didn't want you to see her as she was. I have to say it was a bit grotesque towards the end. She wanted you to remember her as a healthy woman.'

'I could have been a comfort to her.'

He said nothing.

After I had recovered my stability a little, I said 'What do you do now?'

'I finished high school last year, just after she died. I've got a job at the local supermarket. It's keeping me alive at least.'

'But what do you want to do? You can't stay like that for ever.'

'No,' he agreed. 'I'd like to go to university. I'm saving my money.'

I looked at this fine young man, the son of two good people who had both suffered tragedies, and who had had more than his share of hardship already.

'Can we visit her grave?'

'Of course.'

It was a bleak, windy day and we didn't stay long. I put some flowers on her grave and stood for a while in silence, thinking of what might have been.

'I can't do anything for her now,' I said, turning to her son. 'But I am hoping I can be of some use to you.'

'How do you mean?'

'I have some money put aside. I can give you a loan to pay for university. Repayable at any time, of course, with no interest.'

He hesitated. It was obvious he didn't want to appear too eager to say yes.

I pressed the point. 'I live a simple life,' I said, 'and I'll never get married now. I really would like to help you.'

He smiled and nodded in acceptance. 'Thank you. Thank you very much.'

And standing there at Madeleine's grave, I felt, for the first time, a sense of fulfilment.

There was someone who needed me.

And whom I needed.

Avoca Place

It was a quiet, short cul-de-sac, called Avoca Place. Just five houses on it. No one ever came except the people who lived there, and the postman who rode up and down it in two minutes: and that was the highlight of the day.

He came, riding on his bike so that the letter boxes were on his right hand side, and got to Number 2 first. These people always had mail, he grumbled. Even on the slackest day there would be something for them. They were a young couple, still in the 'before children' stage, and madly saving to pay off the bulk of their mortgage before starting a family. They had investments, it seemed. They were always getting annual reports and stockbrokers' reports. Their names were Fisk. The postman, who had never met them, didn't like them.

Number 4 was Mr Lowry, retired, who spent all his time in the garden. He was either mowing, or weeding, or planting, or pruning, or trimming, or adjusting his sprinklers, or sweeping non-existent dust from his footpath, or spraying for non-existent pests, or looking for non-existent snails, or worrying about birds coming to defecate on his driveway. He was always working, working in his garden, and never seemed to be able to take the time to actually enjoy it. The postman had never seen him sitting in the shade of his immaculate tree enjoying a drink. He would nod contemptuously to the old man, who didn't get much mail, and carry on.

At the furthest end of this small cul-de-sac stood Number 5. At the moment it stood empty, and that suited the postman fine. Because he could ride across the little grass island in the middle of the road, straight on to Number 3.

Number 3 housed Mr and Mrs Worthington and their young

daughter Susan. The postie didn't know much about them. The house and garden were normal in every way and they only got their fair share of mail. *Boring*, he thought as he rode on.

Number 1 in this short street contained a family of five, the Johnsons: three children in school, and husband and wife both working to raise the kids and pay off the mortgage. The front lawn, unmown, contained a trampoline and a pen containing guinea pigs and possibly rabbits. A few scattered toys surrounded the pen. A small dog would yap at him as the postie stopped to deliver their mail. He contemplated the sort of life that family must have, and wondered if he would ever end up like that. 'No way,' he shuddered, and swung round the corner into the next street.

And every day that was the sum total of the excitement in the street.

Then one sunny day he got a shock. As he rounded the corner into the street, he noticed Mister Lowry, the meticulous gardener, standing at his gate. 'No mail today, Mr Lowry,' he called as he approached.

'That's not what I'm waiting for,' growled the old man.

'What, then?'

'There's somebody moving into Number 5. One furniture van's been already and there's another one coming any minute.'

The postie groaned as he carried on. 'Another house to deliver to,' he said to himself.

The next morning, as he sorted the mail, he noticed a letter addressed to a Miss Silvers at Number 5. *Hope she doesn't get much mail,* he thought.

But his worst fears were soon realised. The new occupant of Number 5 started receiving lots of mail; all of them seemed to be personal letters as opposed to the official reports of the Fisks at Number 2. And they came from all over the country, and even from overseas.

He sighed. 'Bloody penfriends,' he said. 'Hasn't she heard about email and Facebook? Nobody does penfriends these days.'

But Miss Silvers did. The letters poured in, at least half a dozen every day.

It must take her all her time just to reply to them all, he thought. But strangely enough, he never saw her walking out to post letters. He didn't know what she looked like. Her lawn received the occasional mowing from a local boy, and the house was always quiet. No dog barked, there was no car in the driveway, and his curiosity grew.

But things were changing. Mr Lowry didn't seem to be out in his garden half as much.

One morning he noticed a little clump of soil on the driveway and thought, *The old man's getting past it. He would never have let that happen before.*

The mysterious Miss Silvers at Number 5 got her usual half-dozen letters: two from Queensland, one from Tasmania, and one each from Brazil, Holland and England. He sighed. Not only did she get lots of mail but she had a ridiculously small letter box. 'Serves her right if her letters get scrunched,' he said to himself.

The Worthingtons at Number 3 had a registered letter, addressed specifically to Mrs Worthington.

The door was opened by a girl of about six. 'Mummy's sick,' she said.

'She needs to sign for this letter,' he said.

'Come in.'

The girl led the postman to a bedroom where Mrs Worthington lay with a single sheet over her and covered in sweat.

'I think I've got pneumonia,' she said.

'Can you sign for this letter?'

'Yes.'

'Have you called for a doctor?'

'No. We can't afford one.'

'I'll call for one now,' he said, reaching for his mobile phone. 'You need attention. And don't worry about the money. Medicare will cover most of that.'

'Thank you.' She seemed very weak.

'What about your husband?'

She lowered her eyes. 'He's not around any more. There's just me and Susan. This letter is from him, probably filing for divorce.'

He didn't quite know what to do then. 'Look,' he said, 'I've got to keep delivering. But the doctor says he'll be here soon.' He took a deep breath. 'When I've finished my round, I'll come and see how you are. I should be about an hour and a half.'

She nodded thanks and closed her eyes.

He hurried round the rest of his deliveries and within ninety minutes was back at the Worthingtons'. When he knocked on the door, there was no reply. He knocked again. Nothing.

Old man Lowry called to him from across the road. 'They've taken her to hospital, mate,' he said. 'Ambulance came about ten minutes ago.'

'Thanks,' he said, and went away, muttering, 'You nosey old bugger.'

At the local hospital, he was soon standing beside Mrs Worthington's bed. She seemed calmer and cooler.

He felt a bit embarrassed. 'I just came to make sure you're all right,' he said.

She nodded thanks and reached out to hold his hand. 'Could you do me a big favour?' she asked.

'Of course.'

'Susan went to school after the doctor came. When she gets home could I ask you to bring her here?'

'Sure. But haven't you got any friends who could do it? You hardly know me.'

'No,' she said. 'Since our marriage started to break up, all our so-called friends have kept their distance.' She continued holding his hand. 'What's your name? I've only ever called you "postie" before.'

'Rick.'

'I'm Isabella.'

'Right, Isabella. I'll bring Susan back here soon.'

And as he walked out, he thought, *What a turn-up!*

When he got to the primary school at finishing time, there were difficulties.

'We can't let a young girl like that go with a man she doesn't know,' said the security man.

'I'm her postman.'

'I don't care if you're her bloody priest. You're not taking her away just like that.'

'Let's phone her mother. She's in hospital. She'll vouch for me.'

And Isabella Worthington, already starting to feel better, was able to tell the security man that it was okay for Rick to bring the girl Susan to her bedside.

'Fair enough, mate,' said the man. 'But you can't be too careful these days.'

As they stood by her bed, Rick said, 'What's going to happen with Susan tonight? Will she be able to stay with you here?'

'Yes. I've arranged that.'

Rick smiled at her. 'You're starting to look better already.'

Within three days, Isabella Worthington and her daughter Susan were back home.

Things seemed to settle into their old routine. The Fisks at Number 2 continued to receive their investment papers. Mr Lowry seemed to be out in his garden more often again ('I just had a bit of a cold,' he said), Miss Silvers continued to get her penfriend letters, and the front lawn at Number 1 was as untidy as ever.

But at Number 3, Isabella Worthington, now fully recovered from her illness, would often have a drink ready for him, and always called him Rick; while everyone else called him 'postie'.

Now Rick was a normal red-blooded guy and he wasn't slow on the uptake. One day he noticed her garden needed weeding and said, 'I'll come round after I've finished delivering and help you.'

She thanked him and in due time he presented himself, with the afternoon free in front of him and at least an hour before Susan got home from school. He wondered what the hour would bring, and in his fantasies hoped that she would pay him 'in kind' rather than in money. He didn't quite know how to approach that scenario. He knelt and weeded her front border, and when he was finished, they sat on the back deck drinking lemonade in the warm sun.

'How much do I owe you?' she said.

This was the crunch moment, he thought. If he was bold, it could lead on to great things. But he had to be careful; one false word could ruin everything.

'What do you want to pay me?' he said, throwing the responsibility back to her.

'Will twenty dollars do?'

He managed to hide his slight disappointment. 'Yes, sure,' he said. *Maybe I've got to take this a bit more slowly*, he thought.

She gave him the money and he said goodbye, just as the girl Susan came home from school.

How could I have done that differently? he thought, but before he could answer himself, he heard Mr Lowry from across the road calling to him.

'So you do a bit of gardening, eh?' said the old man.

'Just to help her out,' said Rick.

'Want to earn another few dollars?'

Well, why not? thought Rick. *It could be a good little sideline.*

Old Mr Lowry led him round to the back of his shed and said, 'I need a hand to move these rolls of wire to the garden. They're getting too heavy for me. Then I'll need help putting it round my strawberry patch.'

An hour later, Rick was walking out of Mr Lowry's place, tired but another twenty dollars richer, and with the prospect of more work to come. *That's not bad*, he thought. *A bit of extra cash from the old man and still the chance of something extra from Isabella Worthington.*

He walked to his car and then stopped in annoyance. There was a boy, no more than fifteen, leaning against his car and with his bike upside down in front of him.

'What's going on?' said Rick.

'I got a puncture,' said the boy.

'What are you doing here?'

'I've come to Miss Silvers's place.'

'Miss Silvers?'

'Yeah. At Number five.'

'I know where she lives. I'm her postman. What are you doing visiting her?'

'I come every evening. She gets me to take her letters and post them.'

Rick stuck out his chin. 'Does she now? And you come every evening, you say?

'Yes.'

'That's why I've never seen you before. I come through here in the mornings. Does she pay you well?'

'Not really. I don't like it. I'd sooner be home playing on the computer. And I keep getting punctures on this bloody bike.'

Rick touched his arm. 'Tell you what, let's go and see this Miss Silvers. And if she's agreeable, I can take her letters when I come to deliver, and save you the trouble.' Then he grinned. 'And just to persuade you even more, I'll help you fix your puncture.'

Miss Silvers turned out to be a surprise, and – Rick had to admit – something of a disappointment. She was seventy if she was a day. And she walked with a decided limp. But she smiled at the two young men and agreed that it would be better all round if she left her outgoing letters for Rick to take back to the office.

'Why don't you use email instead of all this mail? It must get expensive,' said Rick, vaguely aware that he was promoting an institution that was in opposition to his job.

'Email?' she said.

'I'll show you how to use it,' said the boy. 'Where's your computer?'

'Computer?'

Rick and the boy looked at each other. 'What's your name, mate?' asked Rick.

'Tony.'

'Well, Miss Silvers,' said Rick, 'I can take you down into town and me and Tony can help you buy a good simple computer. Once you get the hang of it, you'll find it much better to keep in contact with all your friends rather than the mail.' And again he felt a slight unease that he was batting for the enemy.

'Well, I don't know,' she said. Then she smiled. 'But I'll tell you one thing. I'll make you both a cup of tea while I think about it.'

'Thank you, Miss Silvers.'

'Please call me Elaine.'

As they sat over their tea – and scones that Elaine Silvers produced – Rick said, 'It's too late today to go down the shops now. Tony, can you make it tomorrow afternoon after school?'

'Yes, sure,' said the boy.

'If you're still agreeable, then, Elaine, we'll do that.'

'And,' said Tony, 'if you're still not sure, you can hire a computer for a month to see if you like it.'

Elaine Silvers walked out with them, and Rick was suddenly reminded of another thing.

'Elaine, your letter box is really too small. What if I build you a bigger and better one? Would that be all right?'

'How much would you charge?'

'Oh, nothing. It wouldn't be hard. It would just make my job easier.'

The following afternoon saw the three of them in Rick's car heading into town, and not much later there was a simple computer sitting on the back seat.

'I'll show you how to use email,' Tony said.

'Let's celebrate by having a cup of coffee,' said Elaine Silvers.

They sat and relaxed in the nearby café.

'You know,' she said, 'I haven't had so much fun for a long time.'

Sheesh, thought Rick, *you must certainly live a dull life.*

A well-dressed couple came and sat at a table next to them.

The waitress came to them straightaway. 'Hello, Mr Fisk, Mrs Fisk. What would you like today?'

Rick heard her and turned his head to them. 'Do you live at Number 2 Avoca Place?' he asked.

They looked at him, slightly shocked. Who was this upstart asking them where they lived?

'Why?'

'I'm your postman.'

They laughed and relaxed. 'Oh. We've never met you before.'

'This is the new lady who's just moved into Number 5,' he said.

'We don't know anybody else in the street.'

'How long have you been there? You were there when I started.'

'Nearly six years.'

'Well,' said Rick, 'the old fellow next door to you is Mr Lowry. Elaine here is at Number 5. Mrs Worthington and her daughter are at Number 3. And the Johnson family are Number 1.'

They laughed again. 'Well, now we know the names of all our neighbours!'

Rick, the boy Tony, and Elaine Silvers prepared to go.

'Nice to meet you,' said Rick to the Fisks; and to Tony, 'Let's get back and fix up this computer for Elaine.'

They drove back in his car and, as they rounded the corner into Avoca Place, Rick suddenly slammed on his brakes. There was a girl, about eight years old, calmly riding her scooter in the middle of the road. She looked up in fright and scuttled to the side.

'I guess she's not used to traffic on this quiet street,' said Rick.

He was about to carry on when a woman came rushing out from Number 1. 'What do you think you're doing!?' she shouted. 'You nearly hit my girl!'

'But I didn't. And I stopped in time,' said Rick.

'You should be more careful!'

Rick drove on, saying nothing. 'So should the girl,' he said to his companions, and they nodded.

'That was the Johnsons,' said Tony.

'You know them?'

'Their oldest boy is in the same class as me at school.'

'What's he like?'

Tony shrugged. 'He's okay. A good footballer.'

They installed Elaine's computer and Tony educated her in the mysteries of email. By the time they had finished, it was almost dark.

'I'll drive you home,' said Rick.

As they drove out, the girl was still riding her scooter, and standing by the side of the road was a boy of about Tony's age, watching her.

Tony leaned out of the window. 'Hiya, Shaun!' he yelled.

Shaun Johnson looked up in surprise and waved.

'They seem to have taken over the whole street,' laughed Rick. 'Who's the other kid in the family?' he asked.

'Freya,' said Tony. 'She's ten. And the girl you nearly hit is Ingrid.'

'Well,' said Rick, 'I've met almost everyone in the street now.' And his thoughts turned once again to Isabella Worthington. He had arranged to do more gardening for her and he looked forward to developing their friendship.

Two mornings later, he had another registered letter for her.

'This is from Tom,' she said, and seemed a little happier about it.

'Tom?'

'My husband.'

'Are you going ahead with the divorce?'

'No. I don't think so. He's come to his senses.'

'How do you mean?'

'He had an affair with a younger woman and thought he would run off with her. But apparently she's ditched him. He wants to come back.'

'And you will forgive him?' he asked.

'Oh yes. It wouldn't be the first time.'

Rick the postman went away with a definite feeling of disappointment. His hopes of an affair with Mrs Worthington were dashed. That afternoon, he made a bigger letter box for Elaine Silvers and installed it for her. 'How are you going with the email?' he asked as they drank tea afterwards.

'I'm getting the hang of it,' she said. 'It certainly makes it easier and quicker. But I still like the idea of real letters. It's more romantic somehow.'

Romantic! *Not much romantic happening in my life now*, he thought sadly. Tom Worthington was coming back to his wife, and there was little else on the horizon.

The following Monday, he was surprised to see a note on the letterbox of the Johnsons at Number 1.

'Please call in, postie,' it said.

Mrs Johnson opened the door. 'I just wanted to say I'm sorry about the other day. I was angry at the time. When you have kids, you'll understand. But you were right, Ingrid should have been more careful.'

Rick laughed. 'That's okay. I'd nearly forgotten about that. The boy who was with me, Tony Collins, told me the names of all your family. He's in the same class as Shaun.'

'Yes.' She paused as if in thought. Then, 'Shaun's having a birthday on Saturday. He's invited Tony. Would you like to come too?'

Rick raised his eyebrows. 'Well, yes. Thank you.'

But before that date came around, old Mr Lowry needed more help in his garden. He was erecting a pen to house chickens.

'I met the Fisks not long ago,' said Rick as they worked together. 'They seemed decent enough.'

'They're very quiet,' said the old man.

'I'm coming round to the Johnsons' on Saturday,' said Rick. 'The boy Shaun is having a birthday party.'

'When's his birthday?'

'On the Saturday. The twenty-fourth.'

'It's my birthday on the twenty-fifth! Just one day after!'

Rick couldn't resist a smile. 'But a different year, though?'

And to his surprise the old man threw his head back and roared with laughter. 'Yeah! About sixty years difference!' he laughed.

Then Rick had a sudden idea. 'Why don't we have a combined party?' he said.

'Oh, I don't know,' said Mr Lowry.

'How long since you had a birthday party?' Rick asked.

The old man folded his arms and thought. 'Many years,' he said. 'Many years. Not since my wife died. My son went to live in America and I've not really celebrated my birthday for a long time.' He suddenly seemed galvanised. 'Let's do it, eh!'

'Yes,' said Rick. 'Did you know that Tom Worthington is coming back? Now it's Shaun Johnson's birthday and your birthday. And Elaine Silvers has just got her first computer, that's worth celebrating. We'll invite the Fisks and make it a street party.'

Mr Lowry stood and looked at Rick the postman. 'Young man,' he said, 'You're doing me a power of good. I just want you to do one more thing.'

'Yes?'

'From now on, call me Sam.'

Rick laughed. 'Okay, Sam. Leave it with me. I'll see 'em all and on Saturday we'll get together for the party.'

'I'll tell you something else,' said Sam Lowry.

'What's that?'

'Be wary of that Tom Worthington. He's a Lothario. This isn't the first time he's run off with a bit of skirt.'

'What's a Lothario?'

Mr Lowry grinned. 'Look it up on your computer,' he said; and Rick grinned back.

It didn't take long for the Johnsons and the Worthingtons to agree to the idea. When Rick spoke to Elaine Silvers, she seemed reluctant.

'I never was one for parties,' she said. 'I always felt embarrassed.'

'Well, you won't be expected to get up and dance or anything like that,' smiled Rick. 'Just sit and chat and meet the other people in the street. You can tell them about your computer.'

She still seemed hesitant but did agree in the end.

'I'll sit with you,' said Rick. 'There's nothing to worry about.'

But when the afternoon came, Rick was in for more surprises. Tony Collins, the boy who had helped them with the computer, came along and brought his sister. And what a stunner! She would have been about twenty, Rick thought, and the phrase 'perfect in every way' came to his mind. *Things are looking up*, he thought to himself.

He sat down next to her, introduced himself, learnt that her name was Briana, and commenced to chat amicably with her. She worked in a haberdashery shop in town, and – Rick learned to his delight – she didn't have a boyfriend. (*Not yet!* thought the young man.).

They were talking pleasantly when suddenly two figures approached them. It was the Fisks, looking slightly uncomfortable.

'We feel a bit out of it,' they said.

'Don't worry,' said Rick. 'Let's go and get a drink. I'll introduce you around.' And turning to Briana Collins, he said, 'I'll see you in a few minutes.'

The Johnson house was serving as the base for the street party, and Rick led the couple to the kitchen where food and drinks were available. Harry Johnson was standing nursing a drink and watching everyone else chatting and laughing.

'Mr Johnson – Harry –' said Rick, 'this is Mr and Mrs Fisk from across the road.' He turned to the Fisks. 'I don't know your first names.'

'John and Debbie,' they said as they shook hands with Harry Johnson.

Rick was anxious to get back to Briana Collins. 'I've been hoping to have a talk to you,' he heard Harry Johnson say to the Fisks as he backed away. He had other things on his mind.

When he got back outside, Briana wasn't there. He looked around and old Sam Lowry caught his eye. 'Where's the young lady gone?' he asked.

Sam laughed. 'I ain't so sure she's a lady, mate,' he said.

'What do you mean?'

'Tom Worthington cracked on to her as soon as you left. I warned you about him. They've gone off somewhere quiet, I reckon.'

Rick stood with his hands on his hips. 'Bastard!' he thought.

He looked again at Mr Lowry. Elaine Silvers was sitting next to him and it was obvious the two had been talking together.

Well, they say it's never too late to fall in love, he thought bitterly. *The way I'm going, I'll be seventy-five before I get a girl!*

He went back inside the Johnsons' house and saw that Harry Johnson and the Fisks were deep in conversation. He heard snatches of words, like 'good investment' and 'just five dollars a month'. He remembered that Mrs Johnson had mentioned to him that they had received a small inheritance and were wondering what to do with it. The Fisks, with their financial expertise, would advise them well.

The younger Johnson children together with Susan Worthington were playing in the front yard; Tony Collins and Shaun Johnson were absorbed in a computer game; Mrs Johnson was happily providing sandwiches and drinks; Elaine Silvers and Sam Lowry were beginning to cement a firm friendship; and Rick stood wondering what to do next.

I've never actually set eyes on this Tom Worthington, he thought, *but he stole my potential girlfriend and I hate his guts already!*

He wondered where Isabella Worthington was. She hadn't been seen at the party. Rick had surmised that she was busy welcoming her wayward husband back, but if so, she had failed to curb his roving eye. *A Lothario!* thought Rick. *A lecher! And a bastard!*

Leaving the others happily intermingling, he walked up to the Worthingtons' house and knocked. Isabella opened the door.

'Are you coming to the party?' asked Rick. 'Everyone's there.'

She had a defiant and determined look on her face. 'Yes, I'm coming to the party,' she said. 'Eventually.'

'Eventually?' echoed Rick.

'That ratbag husband of mine has shuffled off with a young girl again. He can't keep his mind above his waist! The fool!' She looked at Rick. 'But I'll show him!'

'How do you mean?' he asked.

She took his hand and smiled. 'How do you think?' she said, and led him inside.

'Did You Win?'

It's a stupid question, but they always ask it. It's usually done in an aggressive manner, with a deep voice and the corners of the mouth turned down. 'Did you win?'

No, of course I didn't win! I'm no weakling but I'm no champion either. I'm just another weekend warrior, racing on my bike against a hundred others. A hundred opponents! That means I've got a one per cent chance of winning. But that didn't stop them.

'Did you win?' every Monday morning as we sat in the tent before starting the labouring job.

I tried to explain to them. 'Look,' I said, 'There's at least two potential Olympic riders in our races. I've got no chance against them. And there's over ninety other guys besides that. Of course I didn't win!'

They turned their attention to Barry. Barry was not the brightest star in the sky, but he was solid and dependable. He raced pigeons. That was enough for the rest of them to rib him.

'Did your pigeons win?' they asked.

'No,' he replied lamely, and they laughed.

The fact didn't seem to register with them that Barry had at least endeavoured to do something with his life at the weekends, instead of emulating them by sitting around drinking and finding fault with everything.

There were only eight of us in our 'gang'. It was a simple job, digging trenches for electrical cables. I was only there for about eighteen months but I still think about it a lot. I think it's because we were outdoors, which I loved, and the work wasn't too hard. If it rained (and this was England, remember!) we didn't work. And of course, I was young and everything was new, everything was an adventure.

'You know what you want to do wi' them pigeons?' said Don.

'What?'

'Neck 'em!' said Don.

I spoke up. 'Take no notice of him, Barry,' I said. 'He doesn't know what he's talking about.'

'I do!' said Don. 'You should neck 'em an' start again.'

'He's never seen a racing pigeon in his life,' I assured Barry.

'That don't matter,' said Don. 'He's not winnin' any races. Neck 'em!'

All the other fellows were sitting now with silly grins on their faces, enjoying the joke.

Barry remained silent but his face said it all. He was annoyed, if not downright angry, that someone as unqualified as Don should try and advise him about his beloved birds.

The conversation faded away and we returned to our usual subjects of football, fishing and females. The foreman was a keen fisherman but we didn't dare tell him how to fish better.

I was a mad keen racing cyclist and received my share of good-natured ribbing for not winning every race. But when Barry's pigeons came up, he was fair game, because he took seriously what was aimed at him in jest.

Most people learn in the schoolyard how to handle a bit of ribbing. Laugh it off, joke along with the jokers: that's the way. If you take it seriously, they'll only tease you more and more until you end up in tears. You've got to realise that they're just having some cheap fun. But that piece of wisdom seemed to have bypassed Barry. If anyone mentioned his pigeons, he was immediately on his guard. I sympathised with him and ended up offering to help him train his birds. Barry didn't have a car and he needed to get his birds taken some distance away so that they could fly home, which was good training. As a cyclist, I was able to take two or three birds in a small basket on my bike to a spot about twenty miles away and then release them. It worked well. I got some training in, and so did Barry's pigeons.

This continued for some time through the late summer evenings. Then one Monday morning came the inevitable question to Barry about his pigeons: 'Did you win?'

I noticed Don and a couple of others with grins on their faces already. Once again they'd be telling him his birds were no good, that he ought to 'neck 'em', that he ought to start all over again.

But they were in for a shock.

'Yes,' he said. 'Got in just before the second bird.'

That quietened them! 'Curly's training has been doin' some good, then,' they said.

'Yep,' said Barry.

'You should pay him,' said one.

I jumped in quick. 'No,' I said. 'I'm getting my training in too. I don't want paying.'

And there it stayed. The gang had been deflated. They turned their attention to my cycling. 'Did you win?'

I knew how to handle them. 'No,' I said, 'I'm not fit enough at the moment. I'm using these next few races to help me get fit. Give me a couple of months and I'll show 'em.'

But that wasn't good enough for them. 'How come you're not fit enough? You tell us you do lots of training.'

I laughed. 'Too much drinking after work with you guys. It's all your fault!' But I said it jokingly, intimating that it was my own weakness for letting them seduce me into going for after-work drinks with them.

Well, the atmosphere of the gang started to change after that. The next week, Barry informed them that his star pigeon had come a close second; and I told them that even though I hadn't got a place in my race, I was improving. 'I'll soon be up there with 'em,' I said.

They seemed to lose interest. Next week, Barry said that two of his birds had come third and fourth, and they quickly turned their attention to other things.

Then he made a silly mistake. One day he brought in the latest issue of the *Pigeon Racers' Gazette*. No one else was interested in reading it, of course, but I picked it up and idly scanned the pages. It had the results of the latest races. Barry had told us again that his best pigeon had won a race, but they weren't interested now that he was doing well. I looked through the list of place getters in the races, and Barry's name was nowhere to be seen!

I twigged straight away. Barry wasn't as green as he was cabbage-looking after all. His pigeons were still doing no good, but he was telling the men they were doing well, just so's they'd stop chivvying him about it. I had to stifle a smile. But when we were alone I said to him, 'Don't bring that *Gazette* into work, mate.'

'Why not?' he said.

I looked him straight in the face. 'Because your name's not anywhere in it,' I said.

His mouth opened and he blinked. 'Ah, right, yeah.'

'You're not winning any races at all, are you?' I said.

Now he simply looked guilty. 'Well, no, not yet,' he said. Then he gestured to the other workers some distance away. 'But they don't know that. It's got 'em off my back.'

I smiled at his craftiness. 'Yep,' I said. 'But don't bring that paper to work. Someone will read it and they'll realise what you're doing. Then they'll really make your life hell.'

He changed the subject. 'You winning any races yet?' he asked.

'No.'

'How do they know? Tell 'em you win the occasional race and they won't even ask you again. They're only interested in laughing at people.'

Well, he had a point. I decided to try it myself. The following Monday, when they asked me the same old question, 'Did you win?' I said 'No, but I came second.' (I had actually come halfway down the field).

That didn't seem good enough for them until I said, 'The guy who won will end up riding in the Olympics. No one's got a chance against him. So coming second is pretty good.'

I noticed Barry giving me a sly grin. He realised what I was doing. We were both in this conspiracy game together.

And it worked! For weeks, months, Barry and I continued our game of deception; careful not to overdo it. Just the occasional win, the odd place in the top three, and they totally lost interest in our endeavours.

Well, as I said, I was only in the job for eighteen months and I left and moved on to other things. I was young and ambitious and wanted to make my mark in the world. Barry and I lost contact and for many years I forgot all about him.

I moved around a lot, got into other activities, unfortunately fell foul of the law a couple of times, and now here I am.

They give us a daily newspaper and we're allowed to write one letter a week. Most of the guys write to their lawyer trying to get their sentence reduced, or something like that. Me, I don't bother. I have no family to write to, and anyway I'm due out in another nine months. But they've recognised my 'good' behaviour (which boils down to kowtowing to the warders) and they've put me in charge of the library. And to my surprise, one of the things tucked away there is the *Pigeon Racers' Gazette*. For the first time in years, I thought of my old mate Barry.

I looked through a couple of editions and got another surprise. Barry was winning races now! In fact, more than that: he was the leading light of the local pigeon racing scene. President of the association, county representative, and very highly respected throughout the pigeon racing world.

Well! It was time for me to renew our acquaintance. I wrote him a letter, care of the *Gazette*, reminding him of our old times on the gang, and asking him if he'd like to visit an old lag.

In due time, a reply came.

'I'm too far away to visit you,' it read, 'but I can tell you what I've done since our days together. I left that job and got another one where the people were a lot more friendly. They supported me in my pigeon racing and I didn't lie to them. I gradually improved my stock of pigeons and started to really win a few races. On top of that, my wife encouraged me to join the local Toastmasters, and they had courses on how to run meetings. So I joined the County Pigeon Racing Association and eventually became president. I've also built up a good breeding stock of birds and have a reputation everywhere for providing fine racing pigeons. Anita and I had have three children, all boys, and they're doing fine. The oldest one, Barry junior, is getting into pigeon racing now and I think he'll do even better than me. We celebrated our twenty-fifth wedding anniversary not long ago and went to Denmark and Sweden for a good holiday. My birds are still winning races, my three boys are all strong and happy, and I have to say that life is pretty good. Now tell me about yourself.'

Well, what could I say! I could tell him the truth: tell him that on that job I'd discovered the gains to be had from lying, and had spent the last twenty-five years lying and deceiving, making a fortune and then losing it in the casinos, marrying and divorcing in quick order, being convicted of fraud, and spending the last twelve months in here. I could joke about it, saying, 'I spent three-quarters of my money on women and booze: the rest I just squandered.' I didn't know what to say.

Eventually, I decided to do what I've always done. I wrote, 'I was a fairly successful business man, making good money. But then a crooked employee framed me in a fraud sting, and I got sent here. When I get out, I'm going to confront him and clear my name. Perhaps when I get out I can come and visit you, eh?'

I sent the letter off with a chuckle. If Barry was doing so well, maybe I could con him into one of my schemes. Maybe I could make some cash out of him. I laughed to myself often as I waited for a reply. I figured if he could make it, then surely I could.

Eventually, a reply came. I tore it open with eagerness. This could be the start of a new era for me. But his message contained only two words: 'Don't visit.'

And that hit me harder than any warder's baton.

Have You Been Saved?

'Where have you come from?' they said.

'Just out there,' and I gestured towards the desert.

'How did you get here?'

'Give me a drink first,' I said. 'I've been two days with hardly any water.' I drank, courtesy of the generosity of the men in this isolated place. 'I walked here,' I said.

'What?'

I knew they'd want to know more. How could someone walk here? 'I was driving here and my car broke down,' I said. 'I've walked the last fifty kilometres.'

'You should've waited by your car. Someone would come along.'

'I waited for a full day. Not one vehicle!' I sat down and relaxed for the first time.

Outside, the heat bore down. A crow cawed. The wind raised little eddies of dust on the unsealed road.

'I was running out of food and water,' I said. 'I had to make a move. I would've been dingo bait if I'd stayed any longer.'

'Where do you come from?'

'Namminga. One church, one pub, one store.'

'We know that. What were you doing there?'

'Just…living. Nothing special.'

A couple of the men looked at me suspiciously. 'So what made you come here?' one asked in a hard voice. 'Have you escaped from somewhere?'

'No, no, no,' I said.

'Well, why the bloody hell did you come, then? There's nothing here. A few lost souls, that's all.'

'No souls are lost,' I said.

A dog came in, sniffed me and lay down beside me.

I scratched its back. 'I love dogs,' I said.

That seemed to please them.

'Well, at least you're safe here, mate. We'll find a place for you to stay and we'll get out and look at your car.'

'Thank you.'

'When do you have to be back?'

'No particular time.'

'You still haven't told us why you were coming here.'

'I'll answer that by asking you all a question.'

'Yeah? What's that?'

I looked at them all and drew a deep breath. 'Have you been saved?' I asked.

Well! That was like dropping a stick of dynamite amongst them. Most of them just turned and walked away – almost ran! – and went back to their drinks. But one man stayed with his eyes fixed on mine. He had a black beard with little flecks of grey already appearing. I judged him to be about forty.

'You're a religious fanatic,' he said.

'I'm a missionary.'

He leaned back. Everyone else had gone. 'We've never had any missionaries here before,' he said. 'How many converts do you think you'll get in this godforsaken place?'

'No place is godforsaken,' I said.

'Well, you'll get lean pickings here. William's a Baptist, although he doesn't get the chance to go to church here. You'll never convert him to your denomination. His missus follows some sort of Aboriginal faith, and everybody else is probably atheist. We don't talk about religion.'

'Are you an atheist?' I said.

We were sitting side by side now.

'Yeah,' he said. 'I reckon I would be. I don't go in for all that churchy stuff, singing hymns and saying mass, and God knows what.'

'That's not necessary,' I said. 'What matters is –'

'Forget it, mate! Forget it! You want a bed here? You want to stay a few days? You don't want to get into any fights? Then drop the religion talk. You're lucky you're alive! Be grateful for that. Now come with me and I'll show you where you can doss down until you decide to get back to your churchy friends. Where do you come from again?'

'Namminga.'

'Yeah. Well, you can recover and then head back. No converts here.'

'And what is your name?'

'Paul.' He paused. 'When you've recovered, I can take you and we can look at your car.'

'Thank you.' The whole ordeal suddenly was starting to take its toll. I leaned forward and put my head in my hands. I felt his hand in the small of my back.

'You'll be right, mate.'

'Thank you for your kindness,' I said. 'I think I'll have a lie down.'

'Come with me, then. I'll show you a bed.'

The little room seemed dark after the glare of the sunlight but I was grateful to just flop down.

'I'll see you tomorrow,' said Paul.

I nodded in thanks. And then oblivion.

When morning came, I kept my eyes closed. I wasn't eager to meet the new day. I rolled over and slept again. And when I woke, there was a figure leaning over me. My eyes were still half closed but I sensed that this was not a man. Not Paul. This was a woman. The first woman I had seen in this place.

'How are you?' came the voice.

And I knew straightaway that she was Aboriginal, even before I saw her.

'Who are you?' I mumbled.

'Muri,' she said. 'I'm William's missus.'

'William?'

'Yeah. He the only religious one in these parts, mate. He a Baptist. But that don't worry me.'

'Ah yes, William. Paul mentioned him.'

She brought me a drink, which I gulped down. My body was still thirsty from my time in the desert.

'Where's William now?' I asked.

'Down the mine,' she said, surprised. 'Everybody's down the mine.' And she said it as though I was stupid not to know that.

'What do they mine here?'

'Tin.'

'They get much?'

'Nah. If they got lots, there'd be more people here. Hardly any tin down there now.'

'Then why do they stay?'

She sighed, then almost laughed. 'Some people never learn,' she said at length. And again that little derisive laugh. 'Some people never learn.'

I looked at her more closely. She couldn't have been more than twenty-five, and in that light blue dress she moved with an easy athleticism that a white woman could never match, not even after years of training.

'You got children?' I asked.

She laughed again. 'Not yet. Me and William only been together twelve months.'

'So…you're not officially married?'

'Nobody officially married 'round here, mate. Nobody to marry us.'

'I can.'

She looked me in the face then and her eyes widened. 'Can you?'

'Yes. I'm a missionary and I'm qualified to perform marriages.'

Her mouth opened and she sat down in front of me.

'Do you really want to marry William?' I asked. Now I was being bold. 'Or are you just with him for protection? Just with him for the pleasures of the flesh?'

She snorted quietly then. 'You talk funny, mate. "The pleasures of the flesh",' she mimicked. 'Why don't you say it out loud?'

'I'm a missionary and a preacher,' I said. 'I try to make a point of not speaking crudely.'

'Well, you won't make many friends in this town then.'

'I've already made two friends.'

'Who?'

'Paul, who helped me yesterday.' Then I paused. 'And you.'

She recoiled a bit at that. 'You trying to crack on to me?' and her voice was harsh.

'No, I'm not,' I said. 'But let me ask you, why did you come here to wake me up and bring me a drink?'

'Because I know what it's like out in that desert. It will take more than one day to get over that. You need friends to help you recover.'

Now it was my turn to laugh derisively. 'I lost a lot of potential friends yesterday when I told them I was a missionary.' I continued chuckling quietly. 'But I'm used to that.'

'Why you do it then?'

I felt myself moving into missionary mode. 'I want everyone to belong to my religion because I believe it's the right one.'

'The right one?' she asked, and for the first time she had furrows on her forehead. 'What you mean, "The right one"?'

'The right way for people to worship God,' I said. 'The right way to live.'

'You saying there's a wrong way to worship your God?'

'Well, no. Any worship is good, I suppose.' I suddenly felt tired.

'I know the right way to live,' she said, more to herself than to me. 'Around here.'

I lay back. 'I'm tired,' I said. 'I don't want to argue.'

She turned to go. 'Sorree!'

'No, I didn't mean it like that,' I said, and just stopped myself from reaching out to grasp her hand. 'I'm sorry. I'm still tired from my journey here.'

She seemed mollified by that. 'Okay. I'll bring you some breakfast in a while.' She started to leave, but then turned and said sarcastically, 'Yeah, I'm with William for your so-called pleasures of the flesh. Nothing wrong with that. And for protection too, if you must know.' She was almost at the door.

'And love?' I called.

She stopped at the door. 'Yeah, love too. Pleasures of the flesh, protection and love. Pretty good combination, eh?'

She turned at the bright square of the door. I saw the silhouette of her young strong female body through her thin dress.

'And I don't need saving,' she said, and was gone, leaving a square of sunlight behind my closed eyes, with her body planted in the middle of it.

I didn't sleep much then and her remarks played on my mind. She had asked me if there was a wrong way to worship God. No, I had conceded, but it was our conception of God that was so variable.

I knew what I was going to say to her when she came again.

'What does your Aboriginal faith say about God and eternity and the afterlife?' I asked. She had brought me eggs and bacon, and pancakes and milk.

'I'm not a religious person,' she said. 'Don't keep on about it.' But she sat down near my bed and said, 'I guess we acknowledge the power of nature. The wind and the sun, and the rain when it comes. We always grateful for the rain. So we give thanks.'

'Who to?'

'To nature, I guess. To whatever spirit sends these things.'

'But –'

'I'm not talking about it any more!' She rose to go.

'Wait a moment,' I said. 'What about William?'

'What about him?'

'What's he like?'

Her eyes narrowed slightly. 'Why you want to know?'

'It seems he's the only other religious one around here,' I said. 'I thought we might have an interesting conversation.'

'Oh, forget about your bloody religion!' she snapped. 'I've had enough!' And she stalked out.

It was time for me to get up. I dressed slowly and thought about Muri. Maybe this William tried to push his beliefs down her throat and that was why she was so touchy about it. Well, whatever, I was going to accept Paul's offer of a ride back, and the sooner the better. Nothing going for me here.

I walked out into the heat of the street. There were about a dozen buildings, looking shabby and sullen. It was dusty and deserted, except for one old man squatting on his heels against the side of the pub.

I sat beside him. 'Where's the mine?' I asked.

He turned his face toward me and then I saw that he was blind. But he pointed to the north. 'Up the hill.'

'I might take a walk there.'

'No good up there, mate. There's not much tin. It's hot. It's hell.'

'You used to work there?'

'Everybody works there, or used to. Except the women.'

'I've not seen many women here.

'They keep quiet. They stay indoors outa the heat. Not many of 'em.'

And that seemed to be the end of the conversation. He was the only person out of doors, it seemed. And again I felt tired.

'When do the men finish work?' I asked.

'When they've had enough,' he said. 'They don't work for no employer.'

'Nothing to do until then,' I said to myself as much as to him.

'You could go into the pub and get drunk,' he said. 'If you can stand the beer they got here.'

'I don't drink,' I said, and that definitely ended the conversation!

It was hot and still even though it was only mid-morning. I was bored already.

I tried with the man again. 'Did you make much money when you worked in the mine?' I asked.

'Enough to keep me in this lousy place for the rest of my life.'

Silence then. The timelessness of the Australian bush seemed to have pervaded even this small settlement. A skinny dog lifted its leg against the corner of the building.

'You this missionary man they been talkin' about?' he suddenly asked.

'Yes.'

'Only one god 'round here, mate.'

'Yes?'

He pointed a crooked finger up the hill. 'Tin. That's all that everybody talks about.'

'I heard there's not much tin left.'

'Yeah. They just hanging on hoping to find lots more. Some chance!'

I smiled then in a sort of collaboration. 'Some people just don't know when to quit,' I said.

He said nothing for a long time, and I thought I had offended him by passing an observation on his townsfolk.

Then he spoke quietly, as though he had been rehearsing his next remark in his mind. 'I ain't quittin',' he said. He turned his face to me again, with his blind eyes. 'How old do you think I am?' he asked.

I judged him to be at least sixty-five, but I have learnt from experience that when people ask you that question, they want you to underestimate their age.

'About sixty,' I said.

'I'm eighty-one,' he said. 'I worked in the mine until six years ago when I went blind.'

'You worked in the tin mine until you were seventy-five?' I asked.

'Yep,' he said with pride. 'I'm the oldest man ever to have worked there.'

I didn't know what to say then. 'That's very impressive,' I managed lamely

'And,' he continued, 'I worshipped my god just as fervently as you worship yours.'

'Your god?'

'I told you. Tin. And all that worship, all that work, has made me enough so that I can't afford to leave here.' He said it with a sort of resignation rather than bitterness. 'But I ain't quitting,' he repeated.

'How do you mean?'

'When I went blind, my worship at the tin mine finished. I was ready for my reward.' He raised his head and smelled the dust, the heat, the faint aroma of stale beer from inside the pub. And even I could smell that dog's urine.

'This is my heaven,' he said.

'Your heaven?' I said in surprise.

'I love it here.'

'You said it was a lousy place!'

'Yep. And I love it.'

And for the first time I saw him smile. Was he kidding me? Having his fun with this 'missionary man'?

He turned his face to me again. 'Haven't you ever thought,' he said, 'that some people would prefer hell to your heaven?' He laughed. 'You wouldn't have to worry about swanning around playing those stupid bloody harps. And it's warmer in hell.' He laughed again. Then he got up and, holding on to the side of the building, moved towards the door. 'I'm going inside to drink some of their lousy beer,' he said. He suddenly seemed very intense. 'It's not much,' he said, 'But it's the best we've got. And so I've learnt to love it!'

And he left me squatting in the dust, in the heat, the flies, the stillness, the dreamy timelessness of it all. The skinny dog reappeared and instead of urinating on the corner, it sat down beside me, a substitution for my previous companion. *At least some life forms around here like me*, I thought wryly. And I realised I had never asked the man his name. Shameful, I told myself. As a saviour of souls, I should have done better than that.

I looked up as I saw someone walking on the other side of the road. It was an attractive, dark-haired girl, and she was carrying a young baby. She seemed to be the only other person who was astir at this time of day. I watched her until she disappeared around a corner.

I scratched the dog behind the ear. 'Nice-looking girl!' I observed, and he wagged his tail briefly as if in agreement.

I made my way back to my room and lay down. I must have fallen asleep because the next thing I knew there was the sound of voices from outside. The men were returning from the mine.

It wasn't long before Paul himself came in. 'How're y' goin', mate?' he asked.

'Okay, I guess,' I said. 'I haven't done much.'

'Nothing wrong with that.'

'I was talking to an old man earlier. He's blind. Said he worked in the mine until he was seventy five.'

'Oh, that's old Jimmy Cox. What else did he tell you?'

'He said he'd made enough from the tin to keep him here for the rest of his life.'

And to my surprise, Paul laughed hard at that. 'Ol' Jimmy was having you on, mate. He's like that. He's used up all his jokes on us but you're fresh meat.'

'What do you mean?'

He sat down beside me. 'Jimmy Cox is the richest man in this town – by far. He was the best worker in the mine and he never spent an unnecessary cent. He could live in the big city if he wanted to.'

'Why doesn't he?'

'Because we look after him. If he went to the city, they'd put him in a home for blind people and feed him three times a day like a little kid. We take care of him here. We make sure he's okay, we get his food for him, and we walk him home when he gets drunk. And when he finds himself in the middle of the road, we make sure we don't run him down. He's only been blind for six years, remember, so he doesn't have the heightened instincts of someone who's always been blind. We look after him.'

I changed the subject. 'A girl came and brought me breakfast this morning. Called Muri. An Aboriginal girl.'

'Ah yeah, Muri. That's William's missus.'

'They're not married.

'Does that worry you?'

'I'm qualified to marry them.'

'Well,' he laughed, 'you'll be able to earn your keep here after all. William would probably agree to it too.'

'I haven't met him yet.'

'I'll bring him round. Better still, come and meet him yourself.'

Outside, the late afternoon sun still burned. The dog, lying in the dust, opened one eye when we approached and then closed it again.

I wanted to ask Paul about the girl I had seen with the young baby, but something stopped me. I felt as though I wanted to keep her for myself, to find out more about her in my own way.

'Here's William's place,' said Paul.

He walked straight in and I followed in surprise. *Don't these people even knock?*

'Hiya, William. This here's the missionary man we been talking about.'

William shook my hand. He was a fit, good-looking man, handsome even, and he held himself well, erect but relaxed, like an Olympic athlete. This man could have been a film star; or at least a model. Yet here he was in this outpost, this run-down tin mining settlement, eking out a living scrabbling for tin. And living with an Aboriginal girl!

We sat and drank tea (he accepted without comment when I told him I didn't drink alcohol). Our brief conversations revealed that here was an intelligent, cultivated man. And I remembered that Paul had told me that he was a Baptist.

'Well, I suppose so,' laughed William when I mentioned it. 'I was brought up a Baptist and I've never rejected it, but I've not been to church for years. No churches here.'

'I am qualified to marry you and Muri if you want to,' I said.

'What denomination do you belong to?'

I mentioned my sect, which is generally regarded as slightly unusual but not extreme. He showed no reaction.

'All right,' he said. 'When can we do it?'

'What about Muri?'

'Oh, she's wanted to get married for a long time.'

'Where is she?'

'Chatting with the ladies. They get together for a while in the afternoons. When she comes home, we can arrange the details.'

Paul broke in. 'Don't you have to give prior notice – four weeks or something?'

'No,' I said. 'Not now. Not in my denomination.' And I suddenly put my head between my knees as a fit of dizziness hit me. I obviously had not recovered yet from my ordeal.

The next thing I knew, I was lying on the couch and Muri was bending over me.

'You passed out, mate,' she said.

'How long have I been here?'

'Not long. I came in just as they were putting you on the couch. Rest now. You'll be okay.'

I could hear Paul and William talking quietly in the next room, and I took my chance to speak to Muri alone. 'William wants to marry you and I can do that. Are you sure you want to marry him?'

She smiled then, showing her white teeth against her dark skin. 'Yes, I'm sure. Whenever you're fit enough.'

'Don't you want a big celebration?'

'Oh, yeah. William and Paul will organise that. Everyone will come.'

And they did! All thirty-five of them, the whole population. I counted them: twenty-four white people, seven full Aboriginals, and four who must have been mixed breed. Six children under the age of about fourteen and, of the twenty-nine adults, about an equal mix of men and women. Which meant that only about fourteen able-bodied men worked in the mine. No wonder they didn't find much tin!

They had all come.

Paul and some men had built a big fire in the middle of the street (no danger of passing traffic here!) and as dusk approached, the fire was lit and the townspeople stood in a circle. I had dressed as neatly as I could for the occasion and stood with the fire behind me. William and Muri stepped forward. The people applauded and then were respectfully quiet as the short ceremony was performed. William, this most handsome man, and Muri, this compassionate caring girl, were now officially man and wife.

And the circle – all thirty-five of them – rushed forward, laughing and cheering, and embraced the couple. And me too!

'Onyer, mate!' someone shouted, and my hand was shaken and arms were around my shoulders, all from these rough, crude miners who had come together for this celebration. I felt an emotion then that I have seldom felt before. I suddenly felt as though I belonged.

These people had taken me to their collective heart. Not because I was a preacher (I had enough sense to realise that) but because I had become useful. There were cheers and laughter and I saw two or three couples dancing, whirling around with their arms locked in each other's, and then suddenly everyone was in on the act, William and Muri too – and me too! - one big circle, holding hands and circling left, then circling right, men, women, whites, Aboriginals, children, all mixed together; and someone went 'Whoo hoo!', and someone else replied, and then a person next to me went 'Whoo hoo!' and then we were all doing it, and I went 'Whoo hoo!' too, and it was the first time I have felt a spirit like that in years.

Then William and Muri stepped into the middle of the circle and we all moved in once again, and smothered them in a rush of kisses and handshakes and hugs. I felt a tickle on my cheek and realised I was crying: not from sadness, oh no, but from sheer emotion, from sheer joy at this so spontaneous, unsophisticated outpouring of love.

Love. I can call it by no other name.

Paul and a couple of other men had found a place to sit and called out to me. 'Over here, mate. Come an' have a drink with us.'

I sat down with them. Jimmy Cox was with us.

Blind old Jimmy was given a drink of something that looked revolting, but he quaffed it down, sighed, and leaned back. 'You oughta have a real drink, mate,' he said to me. 'Today's a special day. You won't go to hell for one drink.'

People were still coming up to me and shaking my hand.

'This'll go down in the history of the town,' said someone. 'And we couldn't've done it without you.'

Three or four of them stood in front of our little group. They all had a drink in their hand, and one of them, a small wiry man with a Zapata-like moustache, raised his glass and said, 'To the preacher-man!' And they all responded, 'To the preacher-man.'

There was a big group standing around us now, including William and Muri. I felt obligated to reply, and got to my feet.

'Speech!' they shouted. 'Speech!'

I raised my hand. 'Listen,' I said. 'When I came here' – and suddenly they were all silent – 'when I came here, somebody said this place was godforsaken. I chastised him for saying that, but underneath I thought he might have been just about right. But I've never been so wrong in my life. I have experienced nothing but good humour, and simple kindness, and helpfulness, and – yes, I'll say it! – love!'

'Yeah!' they cheered, and glasses were chinked. 'Yeah! Whoo hoo!'

But I hadn't finished. I raised my hand for silence again. 'Now I'm not going to preach to you,' I said. 'I know how far that'll get me!'

And they laughed.

'But,' I continued, 'You need to realise what you've all got here.' I swept my arm. 'Out there in the big world, they still look down on black people. There's lots of people who would have rejected me for not being a drinker. But you have respect: and that's a rare and precious thing. William and Muri have respect for my denomination and were happy for me to marry them. And you have tolerance. A lot of men, coming home from work, would expect their wives to have a meal ready for them. But here nobody worries. The women get together in the afternoons for a chinwag and come home when they're ready. I think that's great! I tell you, folks, you don't know what you've got. You don't need a preacher-man to come here and spout about Jesus and all that stuff. You've got a community spirit, you look after each other…somebody give old Jimmy another drink!'

And they all laughed. But someone did give Jimmy a drink, and I sat down, feeling slightly embarrassed when they cheered.

People were standing in little groups now, laughing and joking.

William and Muri moved around, chatting to everyone. I leaned back and took it all in.

Then suddenly a young woman was standing in front of me. I recognised her immediately. It was the girl I had seen walking along the road just after I'd been first talking with Jimmy Cox.

'I've got a child I want christening,' she said. 'Will you do it?'

'Of course,' I said.

She produced him. He was a fine-looking little baby.

I judged him to be about nine months old. And on impulse I said, 'Let's do it now!'

'Thank you,' she said.

'Where's the father?'

Her eyes dropped. 'He's dead,' she said. 'He was killed in the mine before Tommy was born.'

'Oh, I'm sorry.'

'It happens,' interrupted Paul. 'We all chip in a bit to keep her going.'

I looked at her again. She really was an attractive young woman.

I turned to Paul. 'Get everyone together,' I said. 'We're going to have a christening!'

And what happened in the next two minutes made me laugh. I recalled how everyone had scattered when I first told them I was a missionary. Now the reverse was happening! As word went round that I was going to christen young Tommy, they came around like iron filings to a magnet.

The ceremony was short and dignified. There was total quiet when I said the words 'I name you Thomas Christofferson. In the name of the Father, and of the Son, and of the Holy Ghost. Amen.'

I had expected raucous cheers then, and more 'Whoo hoos', but again I was wrong. They came forward quietly and embraced the girl – Paul told me her name was Caitlin – and shook my hand once again.

'This is amazing,' I said.

'What do you mean?' said Paul.

But I didn't know how to put it into words. I looked at Caitlin and she looked at me, and she smiled. Someone else had little Tommy; she shook my hand and put her left hand over mine, and her touch was warm and vibrant.

'Thank you so much,' she said. Her eyes were big and brown and beautiful, and she squeezed my hand gently before turning to take her baby again.

And for the second time that day I felt an emotion I have seldom felt before.

I turned to Paul. 'Do you think you could get me a drink?'

'Sure, mate. What do you want?'

'Get me a beer, eh?'

'A beer?' he said in surprise.

'Just a light one. It's time to celebrate. Oh, and Paul, could you get a nice little drink for Caitlin too? Bring it to me and I'll give it to her.'

He stood for a moment before moving off to get the drinks. We looked over to where Caitlin was and we saw that she was looking at me.

Paul grinned. 'Sure thing, mate,' he said.

He brought the drinks and I moved towards Caitlin with them. I smiled at her and she smiled back.

'I think I've been saved,' I said to myself as I gave her the drink.

Hot Chocolate

'Would you like a glass of water, Mister Bennett?' I asked.

'Oh, yes please, Billy, thank you.'

I got a glass of water for him, took the chance to have a drink myself, and brought one, of course, for Dominic.

'Thank you, Bill,' said Dominic.

I'll give him that: he always said please and thank you and he always called me Bill, while everyone else called me Billy. I don't mind, either way.

'Hottest day I've known for years,' gasped Mr Bennett.

The sweat was pouring off him. He'd taken his shirt off, as all the vets do on a job like this, and I was bare-chested too. Only Dominic wore his top, and that was soaked through.

'Radio reckons it's over forty,' said Dominic.

'Yes. And it's a lot hotter in here.'

'In here' was the large tin-roofed stable area put aside as the official hospital for the horses. That included occasions such as this, when one of our prize mares was about to give birth.

'Here she comes,' said Mr Bennett. 'Here she is! What a beauty! There you are, Dom.'

Only people like the vet dared to call the head stableman Dom. We all called him that behind his back, of course, but to his face he was always Dominic.

'Have you thought what to call her?' asked Mr Bennett.

'It's a bit of a tradition in our stables not to think of a name until the foal is born,' said Dominic.

The newborn foal was already struggling to its feet and searching for its mother's milk.

'I've got a suggestion,' I said.

Dominic and Mr Bennett both turned to me. I could see the look of disdain on Dominic's face. Who did this young upstart think he was to suggest a name for our latest addition to the stables?

'She's a lovely chocolate colour,' I said. 'And she was born on the hottest day this year. Why don't we call her Hot Chocolate?'

A smile came over Mr Bennett's face and even Dominic turned up the corners of his mouth.

'What do you think, Dom?' said the vet.

Dominic's a fair man, after all. 'Yes,' he said. 'That's a good name. Thank you, Bill. Now clean up here while Mr Bennett and I do the paperwork.'

'You going to have a celebratory drink?' I heard the vet say as they walked away.

'No,' said Dominic. 'I never drink in front of the horses. They can tell, and they don't like it. I think it diminishes their trust in me.'

I cleaned up after the birth. It's a job I didn't like any more than my regular chores, which consisted almost totally of cleaning out the stables of this big racing complex. I should have been proud to be employed by one of the biggest and most successful stables in the country. But I wanted to do better things than cleaning up all the time. I wanted to be a jockey. That's what I'd signed on for. I'd ridden horses all my life, back on the farm, but being a real jockey was what I wanted.

'You'll serve your apprenticeship like everybody else!' said Dominic when I approached him about it. 'When you're ready for riding, you'll be given your chance.'

'And when will that be?'

'When I decide,' he said.

Dominic ran a tight ship, took nonsense from no one, and always made sure we did our jobs properly. He insisted on being called Dominic, as I've said, and he always called us by our proper first names, never any nicknames, and he never actually swore at us, even when he was obviously displeased at something we'd not done right. But so old-fashioned! So rigid!

And I was young and impatient. I wanted to be a jockey, dammit! And this man had me doing these menial jobs all the time. Of course I knew I had to do some of that. There's an old saying amongst jockeys: 'You've got to shovel their shit before you can ride 'em.'

Well, I'd done enough shit shovelling. I'd been there long enough, I reckoned, to be given a chance to ride. But Dominic was having none of it.

So I resigned. Just like that. Handed my notice in and walked out. That showed 'em, I figured.

But I had a lot to learn about life and the workforce. It is not always a nice place. I got a job at the local supermarket, packing bags and collecting trolleys. Then I got a job as a labourer, but because I'm so small the foreman rode me mercilessly, made me the butt of his jokes and gave me the worst of the jobs. When I left, I was sporting a black eye, and the foreman was sporting some very tender genitals.

Being unemployed is the worst of all. I don't know the statistics, but I wouldn't mind betting that a good majority of suicides are by unemployed people. Not that I ever contemplated that. But the hard times made me think about my life and what I really wanted. The one thing I figured out was that horses were my life.

It was time to go back and apply to be an apprentice jockey again.

It was back to the old routine. If I wanted to become a jockey, I had no choice. I shovelled up the manure each day and carted it out to a huge pile, where keen gardeners would come and take it away.

And while I'd been gone, Hot Chocolate had grown up. I felt a great affinity for her, seeing as I had given her her name. Whenever I got the chance, I would go and talk to her. We had some good conversations. Now that may sound a bit strange, whacky even, but if you've lived around horses you'll understand. You get to know them, read their body language, and even recognise different expressions on their faces. I know non-horsey people will snort in contempt at such statements, but it's true. And of course, every sound that the horse makes has a different connotation.

Hot Chocolate was a very intelligent horse. And I know she liked me. She was put through all the usual training rituals, like getting used to wearing a blanket, then a saddle, and being taken out by a trainer to just walk around, exercising gently, helping her to grow stronger.

She was nearly a year old by this time, but still a bit too young for the arduous regime of hard training and racing.

'She's not ready for riding yet,' said Dominic.

'When will I be ready for riding?' I asked. I was getting impatient again.

'Not yet,' he said.

'I'm sick and tired of shovelling bloody shit!' I said. 'I want to go on a training ride, at least!'

'Just be careful of your language, Bill,' he said. 'You'll get your chance in due time.'

Well, that was all right for him! He was doing what he loved. I knew I would love riding if only I got the chance.

It was one year, to the day, since Hot Chocolate had been born and I had named her. I figured she was strong enough to be ridden now. I'm only small and light anyway, even for a jockey.

The horses are taken out for their training very early in the mornings, when there is often a mist and sometimes a frost still on the ground. On this particular morning, it was very misty. All the other horses were out with their riders and you couldn't even see the far side of the training ground.

'Right, girl,' I said. 'This is where I show them what I'm made of.'

And I saddled her up, opened the stable door, and mounted her. For the first hundred metres or so she was okay. I figured she was so surprised at what had happened that she just went along. But when I dug my heels in, she reared up and suddenly I was on the ground with a searing pain in my shoulder. Hot Chocolate turned and came back to me. She nuzzled me and whinnied in concern.

Just then one of the other jockeys cantered up. 'What's going on, Billy?'

'I think I've broken my collarbone,' I gasped.

'You been trying to ride Hot Chocolate?'

It was too painful to nod. 'Yes,' I said.

'You'll cop it from Dom!'

'I don't care if he sacks me as long as he gives me a bloody painkiller first!'

'Come on, mate, let's get back to the stables. Can you walk?'

'Yes,' I said. 'But don't touch me.'

Well, to say that Dominic was displeased was an understatement. He gave me a quick painkiller, made sure that Hot Chocolate was okay, then drove me to the hospital. And every second of that journey he gave me the biggest and loudest and strongest tongue-lashing that I've ever had. And I must admit, now, that it was deserved. But at the time all I wanted to do was collapse into a bed.

Dominic came to visit me every day after work. He never smiled. Dominic wasn't the smiling type. But he came. Every day. Even on his days off.

And my shoulder healed.

I had fully expected to be dismissed but when I was well again Dominic told me to report as usual. It was back to the same old job.

At lunchtime on my first day back, the jockeys welcomed me. 'You gonna have a celebratory drink?' asked one.

'No,' I said, 'I don't want to drink in front of the horses. They can tell.'

But the first chance I got, I went to see my old friend, Hot Chocolate. I'm sure she whinnied with delight when I came to her.

'You're my girl,' I said.

Just then Dominic came in. He stood and looked. 'You're her boy, all right,' he said.

I smiled in agreement.

'When I think you're ready, I'll give you a go on her,' he said.

'When will that be?'

That hard look came over his face again. But not too hard. Hard, yes, I saw. Hard, but fair.

'When will that be?' I repeated.

I swear the ghost of a smile crossed his face. 'It shouldn't be long,' he said, 'but you know what they say: you've got to shovel their shit before you can ride them.'

I raised my eyebrows at his mild profanity and then grinned. 'Yep, okay. Give me the shovel then.'

I Will Make You Fishers of Men

Part 1

I'm stuck in here now. I can't move very much and I don't want to. I spend a lot of time sitting in my chair and looking out of the windows. What I see there often fascinates me. I look out of the eastern window and like to see the sun rise over the lake and chase away the early morning mists. The waterbirds wake and fly away. I sit and watch – and if I concentrate I can actually see them – the mosquitoes and other small insects rise up as the morning warms. Then the swallows will come swooping low to catch the insects.

Occasionally, I see a splash where a fish has risen up to catch an insect. And I ponder on the fact that it's as well that insects breed like – well, like flies! – because they provide the food for so many other life forms.

If I continue to watch, sometimes a man will come to the lake, climb into a rowing boat, and head into the middle to throw out a fishing line. I feel as though I know him, just from that regular action.

As the sun goes overhead, I grow weary of looking out of the eastern window. It's time for them to take me to lunch anyway, and then my after-lunch nap.

But in the afternoon I wheel my chair over to the western window and wait for the sun to come round.

The view from the western window is quite different. There, the men are working to build an irrigation channel from the lake to the further fields. This of course is a good thing, they say. But in contrast to the peaceful scenes of the morning, the afternoon vista is not happy. The guards are ever attendant with their batons. If a man slackens his pace, he is beaten until he picks up speed again. If he can't do that, he is beaten until he is senseless.

That is what happened to me. And that is why I am in here now, in this wheelchair. It seems I will never be able to walk again. The beating injured my spine. So I am stuck in this hospital building now until the project is finished and the inspectors have gone. What they will do with me after that, I don't know.

I feel like an old man now. The beating and the hospitalisation have taken it out of me.

After the men have finished and gone, I like to sit and watch the sun go down. In fact, I've almost got to the stage where I think it can't start sinking without me.

Sometimes the sunsets are beautiful. And I get to pondering on the meaning of it all.

Sure, the sunrise and the sunset are both glorious. But man's inhumanity to man is only too evident. To see the man on the lake peacefully fishing is a comforting sight. And I remember the fact that Jesus associated with fishermen. Oh yes, we are allowed to read the Bible; and I am intrigued by the character of John the Baptist.

But what about this channel that the men are being forced to dig? Is it going against nature? In years to come, when it is complete and the farmers can grow more crops, will anyone remember the terrible suffering that went into its construction? Will it have been worth it just to feed a few more humans, who are over-running the planet anyway?

The lake, the birds, the fisherman, the sunrise and sunset are all beautiful. But the sight of my old comrades being worked to exhaustion saddens me immensely.

So what is the answer? I don't know. I want the world to be serene and peaceful. But instead it is a struggle for survival.

I just hope that I can continue to appreciate what beauty there is in the world until my end comes.

And having seen the way the world could be, and the way the world is, I can only hope that there really is a system of rewards and punishments in the afterlife.

But in the meantime we are imprisoned here. We are adequately fed – just! – and not ill-treated, at least physically. But there is no friend-ship or compassion or even respect from the staff. We are a nuisance to them, a mere statistic.

One fellow patient I befriended is named Anton. He is about two years younger than me. His leg was broken in an accident and, because of the primitive medical conditions at the site, it did not heal properly. He walks with a limp now and cannot do any manual work.

'I can't spend the rest of my life just sitting here,' he said. 'I'm going to escape.'

I had to smile at his naivety. 'And how far do you think you'll get?' I asked. 'Remember you can't walk fast – let alone run – with your bad leg.'

'I've got to try,' he said. 'I haven't got the mental strength that you seem to have. I'll go crazy if I stay in here.'

I sighed. His assessment of my mental strength was exaggerated. I was struggling myself. I needed a purpose, a reason to keep on living with dignity. 'I'll help you in any way I can,' I said.

He nodded. 'Thanks.'

But two nights later, he was gone without a word to me.

The guards found out quickly enough, of course, and a search party was sent out, but they came back three days later without Anton. They didn't seem too concerned. I think they figured that no man could live alone out in that environment, much less one with a disability like Anton. And it would be easy for them to fudge the paperwork on at-tendances. They would still be getting allowances for a certain number of men, and if there was actually one man less than they said, they would divide his portion between them. If the inspectors enquired too closely – which they seldom did – the guards would just say the man was dead.

I sat and looked out of the eastern window, thinking of my friend and what had happened to him, when I thought I saw something un-usual. Something seemed different, and at first I couldn't put my finger on it. Then I realised. The fisherman was climbing into his dinghy and going out on to the lake, as was his custom, but when I looked closely I saw that his little boat was sitting lower in the water than usual. Surely he'd not caught that many fish? I thought.

Then it came to me, and I had to laugh at the audacity of it. Anton had not gone very far at all. He was lying in the bottom of that boat, lying low – literally – until it all died down. Then he would escape.

And the guards never suspected the fisherman. He started coming occasionally to our camp to sell some of his fish. I got a good look at him then. He was of medium height, with a brown beard and friendly eyes. He wasn't too old, maybe in his early thirties.

He would attend to his business, chat with the guards, and go his way. They seemed to like him. They were getting fresh fish every couple of days, the man was making a modest living out of it, and everyone seemed happy.

I was the only one, it seemed, who knew what was really happening.

He started coming regularly, and even was allowed to chat with some of the inmates. One morning I noticed his little boat was not as heavy in the water any more, and I mentioned it quietly to him.

He smiled at me. 'Sometimes my load is not as heavy…' he paused '…as it should be.' And he looked me straight in the eyes as he said it.

Two days later, he was with us again. A group of us sat and chatted with him.

I took the opportunity to further our subversive conversation. 'I have a broken back,' I said, 'And cannot move much without a wheelchair.'

He looked me in the eye again. 'I have heard people say,' he said, with emphasis, 'that you like to help others.' And with that he stood up and left.

But I had got the message. So this was to be my fate: my reason for living!

I made a point of being friendly to Pyotr, who had recently been hospitalised with a broken arm.

'It will be healed soon,' he said, 'and I'll be forced to go back out and work again.'

'Have you ever thought about escaping?' I asked.

'Yes. But I know that's impossible.'

'Why?'

'Where could I go from here?' he said.

I smiled. 'Anywhere,' I said, and left it at that.

Two days later, he came to me again. He looked around to make sure no one else was listening. Then he spoke quietly. 'Even if I were to try and escape,' he said, 'how would I get away?'

I paused before answering. I wanted to make my answer important. 'Who do we know who is not a part of the camp organisation?' I said.

'No one,' he said quickly.

'Think again.'

Then he realised. 'Only the fisherman,' he said.

I smiled and went away. The seed had been planted. Pyotr must work it out for himself from now on.

About a week later, he was gone. And again the guards did a perfunctory search and then forgot about him. And again I saw the fisherman's dinghy sitting lower in the water for a few days.

When the fisherman came to the camp and chatted with us, he looked at me and smiled. I nodded and smiled back. Anyone seeing that would not have suspected our secret.

My job was to point the way. His job was to help them escape.

It was a while before I spoke to anyone else about escaping. A young man, still in his teens, had come into the hospital and I could see that he was angry with the blows that life had dealt him.

One day he sat with me and whispered, 'How do I escape?'

I was surprised. How did he know that I was the person to speak to about that?

'What do you mean?' I said severely.

He was an impatient man not given to subtlety. 'Just tell me what to do,' he said.

I pondered the situation before I answered him. Was he setting a trap? Was he going to betray me?

And I had to answer myself: that I didn't care. I had nothing else to live for. If the guards found out and shot me, I would die happy in the knowledge that at least I had been of some use to a few people.

'Before you were sent here,' I asked him, 'did you ever go fishing?'

He looked at me in amazement. 'Yes, sometimes,' he said.

'And you caught fish, right?'

'Of course I caught fish!' he said. 'What are you talking about?'

'And sometimes,' I said, 'did a fish escape from your hook?'

'Occasionally, yes,' he said.

I turned my chair and wheeled away. It was up to him to work it out from there.

And a few days later, he was gone.

I breathed easier then. It hadn't been a trap.

But it couldn't last for ever. And it didn't.

Part 2

I should have known. I should have seen it coming. I was a fool. Alexander had a reputation, even among the working men, of being a loner, unsociable and sometimes downright uncooperative.

So I thought it would be good if he was gone. He came to me with that sneaky look and asked for help. Good! No one would miss him. So I gave him the usual heavy hints and left him to work it out. But Alexander was not only unsociable, he wasn't very intelligent. He couldn't understand. He came to me again but I wasn't going to tell him outright to go to the fisherman. He had to use his brains.

He went away and I could see that he was angry. I should have known then. Not that I could have done anything about it, confined to my wheelchair.

So when a guard came and said, 'Come with me!' I knew that I was in trouble.

One thing I can say about the regime: they don't torture you. I am writing this in my cell and tomorrow morning they are going to take me out and shoot me. They haven't tried to make me betray the fisherman. Perhaps they know about him anyway, I don't know. All I know is that the men are on their own now. I cannot help them any more. But I am sure that word has got around about the fisherman who will save them.

I don't know, I can't see into the future. Perhaps the fisherman will save many of them. Perhaps the guards will kill him too. I don't know.

But I leave this document in the hope that someone will find it and tell the world our story.

It is time now for me to lay down my pen. It is almost dawn, and I have only minutes to live. I can only hope that good eventually prevails. But that will require a lot of hard work and sacrifice.

Part 3

The above documents were discovered in the library archives of the Church of Emmanuel in the rural region of Babakiza. Babakiza is noted for its vegetables and its fruit orchards, all fed by irrigation channels from the great lake nearby. The channels were dug by interns of a correctional education camp. The Church of Emmanuel was built by the interns as a memorial to a man who helped many of them to escape and alert the authorities about the harsh conditions at the camp.

The man was a local fisherman who would hide the escapees in his boat until they were ready to flee. The story goes that the fisherman himself disappeared when the authorities came to investigate the camp, and there were rumours that he was seen in many other places after that.

No one knows if it is true or not.

La Belle Dame Dormant

Paris in June can be warm. The Tour de France starts soon, the tennis season is in full swing, and people are heading to the coast to bake on the beaches, or into the mountains to hike in the comparative cool.

Not me. I was on holiday in Paris and the weather didn't really concern me. I'm more of an indoors man anyway. I'd seen all the sights: The Eiffel Tower, Montmartre, the Arc de Triomphe, and spent some sublime hours in the Louvre. That was all fine. But I must modify my earlier statement and say that I was on a working holiday. So one evening saw me attending the ballet: it was *Sleeping Beauty*.

I settled back, looking forward to Tchaikovsky's glorious music and enjoying the beauty of human movement. The girl who played the part of the Sleeping Beauty – *La Belle Dame Dormant* – immediately caught my attention. She was young, probably no more than twenty, perfect complexion, blonde-haired and, well – she was a beauty! But from my point of view, what was more important was that she was obviously a very talented dancer. She had a grace and ease that came naturally to her. This was what I was looking for.

After the show, I went backstage to meet her. I speak very good French. The security man stopped me.

'I wish to speak to Mademoiselle Marie Le Blanc,' I said.

'Why?'

'I am a theatrical agent from Sydney, Australia,' I said, showing him my identity. 'I may be able to advance her career.'

In her dressing room, she sat taking off her make-up, but she was still as poised and graceful as she had been on stage. She smiled and accepted my congratulations on what had been an impeccable performance.

We talked for a long time, and our conversation was continued over a meal in a restaurant.

'If you come to Australia,' I said, 'I'll be able to get you bookings in many ballets. The European ballet scene is crowded but Australia can give you more opportunities to advance and become recognised.'

A slight shadow came over her face and she said, 'So you think I'm not good enough to make it in Europe?'

It wasn't that at all and I hastened to reassure her. 'An overseas tour will be a great thing to put on your CV,' I said, and she nodded at the truth of that.

We settled the deal and I went to work arranging passports, work permits, visas and flight bookings, and within a month Marie was dancing in Sydney.

Other cities followed and Marie was obviously enjoying seeing this new and strange country, so vast compared to her homeland.

'It is so different,' she would say. 'The heat is different, the animals are different and the traffic is different. You drive on the other side.'

Marie trained diligently but ballet facilities were not always available on tour. She would go to a gym to keep fit and flexible, but sometimes she just liked to hire a bicycle. Coming from France, she was used to a cycling culture. But Australian drivers are less tolerant of bikes than Europeans. And the inevitable happened.

One morning I got a call from the local hospital. 'Could you please come to casualty. We have a woman here who is asking for you.'

Marie had been hit and was in the operating theatre when I arrived.

'What happened?' I asked.

'She was caught a glancing blow by a car. It's not life-threatening. But her foot has been injured and the surgeons are working on it right now.'

Her foot! This was serious! If Marie had an injured foot, it would mean the end of her career as a ballerina.

'Will it be a permanent injury?' I asked.

'We don't know yet.'

Marie came out of the operation and I took her back to our lodgings.

'They say it will be about six weeks before I know whether it has healed properly or not,' she said.

'What will you do if you can't dance any more?' I asked. 'Go back to France?'

'No. I like Australia. Even if I can't be a ballerina, I want to live here.'

'But you won't be able to stay here permanently,' I said. 'Your work visa is only for six months.'

'I will be able to stay here if I get married to an Australian,' she said, and looked at me with a smile.

Well, as her manager, I had kept a professional distance in our private lives, but the prospect of being married to this beautiful French girl filled me with pleasure.

Some time later, as we lay together, my mind returned from the ecstasy of the previous hour. 'We can settle in any major city,' I said. 'I have enough connections to be able to earn a living in any of them. But what about you?'

'You may be able to earn an adequate living,' she said, 'But I can make more money for us than that.'

'How?'

'Déshabillé.'

I knew what it meant, of course: undress.

'That's where the money is,' she said. 'That's what I'm going to do.' She laughed. 'One thing is certain, when I'm up there stripping, the men sure aren't looking at my foot!'

'Marie, no!' I said. 'Stripping's a dangerous and corrupt world.'

'It may be corrupt but it is rich,' he said.

'No! I am not letting any wife of mine do that sort of thing.'

'I am not your wife yet.'

'Marie, don't do it! Marry me and you can become my secretary. You can help me in my work.'

'It will still be measly money,' she said. 'If my foot doesn't heal, I am going to be a stripper.'

'I am not marrying a stripper!' I said.

She looked over her shoulder at me. 'Then don't.'

That hit me hard. But I had one last argument to put forward. 'If you don't marry me, you won't be able to stay in Australia for much longer.'

And with that, she threw back her head and laughed. 'You said yourself that it is a corrupt world. A world where people get around that sort of thing. A world of bribes and under the counter deals.'

My estimation of her was crumbling by the minute. She had always been a dedicated dancer. Always charming and always, seemingly, chaste and modest. And now here she was proposing to expose herself in front of slobbering moronic men just to make a lot of money.

'I thought you had nobler aspirations than that,' I said.

She laughed. 'You are a nice man,' she said, 'But you are an awful prig.'

'Well, maybe your foot will heal properly. Then we can forget all this.'

We had to stay in that city for the six weeks. I had to cancel bookings, and I couldn't make rearrangement for future dates until I knew how her foot would heal. It was a busy time and a bad time.

She went to the hospital for her final examination and came back with a smile on her face.

My heart jumped with relief. 'So you're going to be all right?' I said.

'Oh I'm going to be all right,' she said. 'But I can't dance any more. It's stripping for me. I'm going to make lots of money!'

I held my head in my hands. I was virtually in tears. 'Marie, no. Please don't do it. We can have a good life together. Please!'

But she was already packing her things and preparing to leave.

*

I didn't see her again for fully twelve years: but I heard enough about her. She became famous among the people who are involved in that way of life. She toured around Australia taking her clothes off for ogling men, and receiving good money for it.

Her manager – which is a polite word for him – was a big man with a reputation. It is an understatement to say that he brooked no non-sense: the occasional unruly customer had a broken nose to prove the truth of that. But he kept her safe, I will say that for him.

After Marie and I parted, I stayed celibate for a long time. But natural instincts will have their way and I eventually married Jodie, whom I had employed as my secretary. It was a disaster. From the start, she showed intolerable jealousy whenever I spoke to an attractive woman.

'You're chatting with that silly young girl again!' she would screech at me.

'That is inevitable,' I would say, 'if I am to be her agent.'

But Jodie couldn't see that. She accused me time and again of infidelity.

One night after a show, I spent an unusually long time speaking to a promising dancer, and when I got home I was met with a barrage of accusations. I told her she was demented, and she stormed out. That was the end of our marriage. We were divorced some months later, and I lost contact with her altogether.

And an inescapable sadness would come over me whenever I thought of a possible romance again. I came to the conclusion that there was only one real love in my life, and I had lost that many years ago.

Then one winter's morning I was working in my office when I heard a commotion outside. My secretary was trying to persuade a man to wait until she spoke with me. But he was having none of it.

He burst into my office and said, 'Where is she?'

'Who?'

'You know who! Where is she?'

It was then I recognised him. He was Marie's 'manager', her protector, and – I wouldn't be surprised – probably her lover.

'You mean Marie?'

'Of course I bloody mean Marie! Where is she?'

'I've no idea. Why, what's happened?'

'She said she's quitting stripping and going back to ballet. Stupid bitch! Just because I told her she was getting a bit old for it!'

'Well she's not come here.' I stopped short of calling him 'mate'.

He paused and then spoke quietly, threateningly. 'If I find out you're lying, you'll regret it,' he said.

'I've not seen her since she left me,' I said. 'I don't know what she's doing or where she is.'

He seemed satisfied with that. 'I'll find her,' he said. 'I'll get her back stripping!'

This was a dangerous man. I had no desire to get on the wrong side of him. He left his phone number and told me to call him if I learnt anything.

I tried to forget the incident. But I couldn't get her out of my head. Twelve years of stripping must have changed Marie for the worse, I thought. I wanted to remember her as she was, playing the part of the Sleeping Beauty. I had completely got over my failed marriage but I had never really forgotten Marie.

The man called again about two weeks later but I had no news for him. He was as intimidating as ever. I trembled for the well-being of Marie if ever he did find her.

But I had work to do. I made a decent enough living, I suppose. I shouldn't complain. But being a theatrical agent meant a lot of late hours. Very often I was still awake after midnight if I had been to the theatre.

On this particular night, I came home from a performance of *La Bohème* – another story of lost love – and I was feeling wistful and melancholy. I made myself a hot drink before going to bed when suddenly I heard a noise outside. What was this at such an hour? Then my door opened and I heard someone come in. I cursed for not having locked up yet. Was this the big man who had come to threaten me in my own home?

Then the surprise of my life! Marie!

'Marie! What are you doing here?'

Her hair was unkempt and she had a hunted look in her eyes. Twelve years of stripping had taken their toll.

'Hide me,' she said. 'Hide me!'

'What?'

'If he finds me, he'll beat me. It won't be the first time. Hide me, Paul, hide me, please. Please! You're the only person I can turn to.'

'Is he near?'

'Not now. But I know he comes here looking for me.'

'Sit down,' I said. 'Calm down. I can hide you if no one saw you come here.'

'I was careful about that,' she said. 'But I can't go back to him. I don't want to go back!'

'You don't?'

'I'm finished with stripping,' she said. 'He told me I was getting too old. Too old at thirty-two! He said he could get two more years out of me, as though he was speaking about an old second-hand car.'

'All right,' I said. 'All right. I can put you in a room. At least he's never searched the house before. But what are you going to do?'

'I want to go back to France now,' she said.

'What about passports and everything?'

She looked at me with her big eyes and my heart melted. I knew then that I had never stopped loving her.

'Yes,' I said. 'I can arrange that. But meanwhile we must hide you. It's too dangerous for you to stay here.'

I thought for a while. Then I said, 'I have access to one of the main theatres in the city. It has lots of small rooms, some of which are hardly ever used. We can hide you in there. My going in and out of the theatre won't look suspicious, and I'll be able to get you a disguise from the props.'

'Yes,' she said. 'But let me stay here for tonight.'

'Of course!' I replied.

And that night our love was confirmed. We lay and talked for a long time, and made the big decision: I would come to France with her. For the first time in years, I rejoiced in my heart. My future looked bright at last.

The next day, I went to the theatre alone but soon returned with a wig, glasses, a dirty overcoat and extra clothing designed to make her look like an old woman. We made separate ways to the theatre and Marie was ensconced in a small room, to stay there for about ten days until our flights were due out of Australia.

Those ten days were hectic. Not only did I visit the theatre every day, but I had to make all the arrangements for our departure. On top of all that, I did as much as I could to offload my clients on to other agents, and all the while keeping an eye out for our nemesis. I hadn't seen him for a long time and I wasn't sure if I could keep my nerve if he confronted me again. I am not a good actor: that is why I became an agent.

But ten days later, we were at the airport. Marie wore a dark wig and glasses. We had not seen the big man but we wanted to be careful. We passed through the airport security gate and took one last look back at Australia.

And there! There he was! And he was looking at us!

My heart jumped and then I realised my folly. I had taken the trouble to disguise Marie but I had not disguised myself. And it was only logical that he would be watching me, especially once he learned – as I'm sure he had – that I was leaving the country.

Was he going to follow us? Then I got a surprise. He looked straight at me, looked straight at Marie – and I'm sure he recognised her – then just shook his head and walked away.

Marie had seen it all. 'He got what he wanted out of me and now he's moving on to new flesh,' she said. 'He doesn't think I'm worth the effort any more.'

'You are worth the effort to me,' I said, and her eyes moistened as she smiled.

We live in Paris now. The roles have been reversed a little. I married Marie, which enables me to stay in France. And I have built up a good reputation here as a theatrical agent.

Marie has become a ballet instructor and her reputation is growing. She incorporates some of the moves she learnt as a stripper into her work and has received many accolades for her innovations. If only they knew where she got them from!

She is doing what she was born for, and now in her mid-thirties she has blossomed into a maturity that still takes my breath away. She is gorgeous!

Between us, we are writing a ballet. We wondered what to call it until we both came up with the same idea. We will call it *Love Is Lovelier the Second Time Around*.

Mirror Mirror

'Jeez, you're beautiful,' he said, looking at the mirror. 'It's a wonder you're not in all the magazines.' He brushed his dark hair back and felt his chin. Just enough stubble to make him look sexy. He looked at the mirror again. 'Mirror, mirror on the wall, who's the best-looking of them all?' he said. And answered himself, 'You are!'

Mrs Ponsonby would be here soon. He was looking forward to meeting her.

Mrs Ponsonby always called round on Wednesday afternoons, at four-forty-five sharp, and Wayne knew that no one was likely to disturb them at that hour, just a few minutes before closing time.

He looked at the mirror again. 'She won't be able to resist you,' he said, and chuckled to himself.

As four-forty-five approached, he grew increasingly nervous. But he steadied himself. 'Mrs Ponsonby always enjoys her little visits,' he thought. 'I've never disappointed her yet.'

At precisely four-forty-five, Mrs Ponsonby came in. 'Hello, Wayne,' she smiled. 'What's on the program for today?'

'Hello, Mrs Ponsonby,' said Wayne. 'Come with me into the back room.'

They walked into the back room of the shop and Wayne turned to her. 'I have the most beautiful mirror. You'll love it. Lovely shape, gold border, it will be a great addition to your antique collection.'

Mrs Ponsonby turned to look at the mirror and gasped with delight. 'Oh, Wayne, it's wonderful! What's your price?'

'Well, you know I'm only a struggling antique dealer, but I'll give you a fair price as a friend.' Then his face creased. 'To be honest, I don't know how much longer I can keep going. I'm hardly making enough to get by.'

'Oh, I do hope you don't have to close down, my dear,' said Mrs Ponsonby. 'You've always been good to me. I wish I could help you.'

Wayne smiled wanly. 'I'll wrap the mirror up for you.'

'Oh no,' said Mrs P. 'I can't take it with me now. I'm afraid I'll drop it. I'm getting a bit shaky these days. Look, I'll send my granddaughter around tomorrow to pick it up, and she'll pay you then.'

When she had gone, Wayne muttered to himself, 'The only way you can help me is to buy the shop from me at an exorbitant price. And that's not going to happen, is it!'

Wayne had scarcely opened the shop the next morning when in breezed a young woman who didn't look like an antique collector at all. She was fresh, fair-skinned, probably in her early twenties, and she had a look of mischief in her eye.

'Hi,' she said, 'I'm Tina, I'm Mrs Ponsonby's granddaughter. I've come to pick up the mirror.'

Wayne looked at her and smiled. 'I have it wrapped up here, ready,' he said.

'I've got the money here for it,' said this bright young girl, 'but –' she paused; she had a little twisted smile and her eyes sparkled, 'would you prefer me to pay you…in kind, instead?'

Wayne understood immediately. 'Come with me into the back room,' he said.

In the back room, he turned to her and said, 'To be honest, Tina, I'd prefer it if you paid me the money. For one thing, I'm gay, and for another thing, I'm not making a fortune in this shop and every dollar is precious to me.'

She nodded in understanding. Her eyes scanned the room and she seemed to come to a decision. 'Tell you what,' she said, 'this back room isn't really used very much. Put a heater in, and a massage table, and you could drop a quiet word to your male customers that I'll give them a…massage…in the back room. Most of your male customers have got plenty of money. Between us, we could make a fortune!'

Wayne laughed. 'That's a great idea,' he said. 'And I'll be your protector. It'll certainly stop me from going bankrupt.' Then his face fell. 'But what about your grandmother? What if Mrs Ponsonby learns what you're up to?'

'Oh, don't worry about that,' said Tina. 'It was her who suggested it to me in the first place!'

Nevermore

When the tree was first planted, it grew strong and sturdy. The occupants of the house, an elderly, gentle couple, watered it regularly and fertilised it at the right times.

The suburb was generally referred to as 'well-to-do', the couple lived quietly, attended church regularly, and liked to play classical music on their phonograph.

When they died – within three months of each other and without any children – the whole street turned out for the funerals, and people asked each other who would buy the house now.

The new couple lost no time in informing their neighbours that they had won 'heaps' of money on the lotto.

'Maybe now that we've got some money, things will be better,' she said.

'Hmph,' he said.

'Look at the trees. Look at the flowers. Isn't it lovely! I'm glad we came here.'

'Hmph.'

'We'll work in the garden and make it even prettier,' she said.

'I hate gardening. You know that!'

'Well, I will anyway.'

'You'll do the housework first, and make sure my meals are ready. Then you can indulge your bloody hobby after that.'

'It's lovely, Jack. We can be happy here.'

'Hmph.'

'Isn't that a nice tree!'

'Let's get inside and have a feed. Have we got any beer?'

'You know we have. Gee, I'm looking forward to settling down here!'

'Hmph.'

Jack and Sarah Baudley found it difficult to make friends with their neighbours.

'Fucken snobs!' he observed. 'Talkin' about poetry or politics and shit like that. Don't see 'em down the pub very much.'

'Maybe you'll spend less time at the pub once the baby is born,' she said.

'Don't you start fucken' nagging me!' he said.

'I wasn't nagging you. I'm just saying –'

'Argh, shaddap!' He stormed out. And there, in front of him, was this gentle green tree. 'Fucken' women!' he said to himself. He went to the shed and grabbed an axe. 'Fucken' tree!' And he chipped a piece out of its trunk.

That seemed to mollify him. He put the axe away and went inside. 'How're ya' feelin'?' he asked.

She looked at him with wide eyes. 'All right, I guess.' She seemed a little pale.

'Get us a beer then.'

In due time, the baby was born. They called her Gail.

'I used to 'ave a girlfriend called Gail,' he said. 'She wasn't bad.'

'I wish you wouldn't talk about your old girlfriends like that.'

'Have you got postnatal depression or something?'

'No. But –'

'Forget it!' he said. 'Forget it!' And he stormed out. He stood with his hands on his hips. 'What's the bloody matter with people?' he said.

The tree rustled in the warm breeze. He gritted his teeth and went to the shed, to the axe. Another chip flew off the trunk and caught him on the hip.

He went inside. 'I've got a sore hip. Have a look at it, will yer!'

She looked and saw nothing but a bit of a welt. 'It's nothing to worry about,' she said.

'Nothin' for you to worry about!'

'Nothing that a beer won't cure,' she said with a forced smile and the wisdom of experience.

Gail was a normal baby, which means that she cried a lot and woke up a lot through the night. Sarah developed a haggard look and moved around with shuffling feet. But she loved her daughter and knew that this hard time would pass. She had no time for gardening now and they employed a regular man for two days a week.

Because he didn't work – courtesy of his big lotto win – Jack was around much of the time when Gail would cry. And he would wake in the night when she woke and cried. He became increasingly short-tempered.

'Why don't you sleep in the day when she sleeps?' asked Sarah.

'I can't do that,' he said. It was easier to go down the pub out of the way.

Thankfully, Jack wasn't an alcoholic. Sure, he often came home with more than enough drink inside him, but that at least helped him to sleep soundly for a few hours before he was woken again to the sound of his daughter's crying.

He gritted his teeth and tried to tough it out. But when he said, 'No more kids' to Sarah one day, she at least found the energy to nod 'Yes.'

And when she agreed so readily, he was surprised to feel his stomach go cold. He went outside and sat down. So this was the total sum of his family. And he found himself admitting, for the first time, that maybe he would have liked more children. He'd just never known before how difficult a new baby could be. Was he a weakling to wimp out after one child?

Aagh! It was all too bloody hard! He grabbed the axe and took another chip out of the tree. That tree seemed to represent fertility and strength to him, and resilience and endurance.

He chopped again. 'Bloody tree!'

He persuaded himself it was in the way, that it blocked the view, that it made a mess with its leaves, that it harboured insects, that it was a fire hazard, that it was an eyesore.

He chopped again, and again, until the entire trunk had been ring-barked. That seemed to satisfy him. When he went inside, Gail was sleeping peacefully. He looked down at her innocent baby face and across to his exhausted wife who was snoozing in an armchair.

He sighed. 'Maybe I'll try and sleep now anyway,' he said to himself.

And just as he was nodding off, Gail woke up and started to cry.

The ringbarked tree died. The leaves turned brown, fell, and never came back. They got scooped up when the gardener mowed the lawn. The bark peeled off in long strips and the gardener took them home and broke them up for kindling wood.

The tree, now starkly white against the blue of the sky, had a beauty of its own. It stood out in this leafy, bosky suburb where everything else was green and fertile.

And Gail turned four. And, as a typical four year-old, she questioned everything. 'Why is that tree white, Mummy?'

Sarah felt slightly embarrassed. 'It died,' she said.

'Why did it die?'

'It died because nobody loved it,' she said, giving a sideways glance at her husband.

'Will I die if nobody loves me?' asked the little girl.

'No, of course not,' said her mother. 'And anyway, we love you and so do your friends at kindy.'

'I learnt how to swing at kindy today,' said Gail. 'My friend Louise taught me.'

'That's nice.'

'Can we have a swing here?' she asked.

'I'll ask your daddy. He should be able to make you one,' she said, and muttered under her breath, 'He's got nothing else to do.'

So Jack, with nothing else to do, built a swing and suspended it from a horizontal branch of the dead tree. 'At least it's become useful for something,' he said.

Gail wasn't a tomboy but she had plenty of four-year-old energy. She spent a lot of time on the swing, it was her favourite place, and both her parents found that to be an agreeable arrangement.

'She looks so sweet out there in the fresh air,' said her mother.

'Hmph,' said Jack. At least and at last he was getting a bit of peace and quiet.

Gail grew more confident on the swing. Sarah loved to watch her from the window. And Jack sat around, with nothing else to do, and said 'Hmph' a lot.

One bright sunny afternoon, a raven came to sit on the fence and cawed loudly. Gail twisted on her swing to look at the big black bird; and Sarah, looking from the window, watched in horror as Gail slowly fell, tried to sit up, and then rocketed back as the swing returned and hit her on the head.

Sarah was out the door and to her before she was still! The raven cried and took off with its heavy wings. As it rose, it saw the woman with the child cradled in her arms. There was blood on the child's head and its mouth was open. The raven, with its primitive mind, wheeled away and was gone.

The hospital doctor had bags under his eyes. He was tired: nay, exhausted. This was a bad case. The little girl had brain damage, he knew that. She was in a coma. There was no way of knowing how long she would remain like that. And he had to break the news to her parents.

They were sitting outside the operating theatre now, looking as exhausted as he felt. Well, there was no easy way out of this. He had to put it to them straight.

'Mr and Mrs Baudley, would you come into my office please?'

After he had told them that their daughter was very dangerously ill, and that she was in a coma from which she might never recover, he had one last piece of advice. 'Go and get some sleep.'

Sleep? Sleep? How could they sleep with this hanging over them?

'Can we sit by her bedside?'

'Yes, I'll arrange that. But I advise you to take it in turns while the other one gets some sleep.'

'Yes. Yes. Thank you.'

Jack turned to Sarah. 'I'll take the first shift.'

And she didn't argue. She didn't have the strength.

He sat by Gail's bedside and looked down at her still, pale face. He remembered the remark his wife had made about the dead tree: 'It died because nobody loved it.' Well, this wasn't going to happen to his daughter! He had heard how people in a coma could still somehow sense the outside world and that the message of what they were saying could infiltrate into their brain.

He spoke to his still daughter. 'You'll come out of this okay, Gail. You had a nasty bang but it's getting better already. Your mummy and your daddy love you very much. We're here all the time and we're looking forward to when you wake up. Then we can play in the yard again. Maybe in the summer we'll go to the beach.'

He carried on like this for a while until he could think of no more to say. He repeated the whole thing a few times, but then figured that if her brain was actually receiving these messages, she would know what he was going to say. He took up a children's book and started to read aloud from it. He read aloud for the rest of his time there. When Sarah came to relieve him, his throat was sore, his face was haggard, and he felt sweaty and grimy.

Sarah did the same things. She told her daughter, her beloved daughter, how precious she was. She read to her from the book, and when she had finished that, she took up another book.

And Gail remained still through it all.

Fifteen days. Fifteen days! How long does hell last? It lasted fifteen days for Jack and Sarah Baudley.

And then it got worse.

Fifteen days and fifteen nights of sitting by their daughter's bedside, telling her how much they loved her, reading to her, saying how much they looked forward to their lives together once she recovered. Four hours on and four hours off.

Exhaustion.

Hell.

And then it got worse.

On the morning of the sixteenth day, Jack noticed a slight movement of Gail's eyebrow. He rushed to the nurse, phoned Sarah, and scurried back to the bedside! Her face was now somewhat darker.

The doctor came in and said, 'Let's get her into the emergency theatre straight away!'

Less than half an hour later, the doctor sat heavily on a chair in the theatre and spoke to the head nurse assistant. They were the only two left.

'It's times like this,' said the doctor, 'that I wish I was a postman or a gardener or something like that.'

'Yes,' said the nurse, because she knew what was coming.

'Because then,' said the doctor, more to himself than to her, 'I wouldn't have to go to those two people out there and say what I've got to say.'

Jack and Sarah sat and held hands.

'Maybe this is the end of it,' she said, and he nodded in high hope.

And it was.

The doctor came out and, once again, called them into his office. And when he said what he had to say to them, Jack Baudley collapsed. They called assistants and carried him to a bed. They gave him tranquillisers and told Sarah she could stay with him. She lay beside him and stared at the ceiling. There were no tears from her. She was beyond that.

Little Gail Baudley was buried in a small plot in the local cemetery. The priest tried to say a few words of comfort which were absolutely useless, and they drove home.

For the first time since her accident, they seemed to notice their surroundings. The tree had fallen down! And their next-door neighbours, Eddie and Virginia Allan, were waiting for them.

'What happened to the tree?' said Jack.

'We had a big gale. It blew quite a few trees down. Did a bit of damage around town. What will you do with it?'

'Don't know,' said Jack. 'That's been the least of our worries lately.'

But the only thing that happened with the fallen dead tree was that the gardener sawed it into manageable pieces and took it home for his fire.

'We're going to have to let the gardener go,' said Jack one day.

'Why?'

'We've got no money left.'

She stared at him open-mouthed.

'I'm going to have to get a job.' He sat down. 'Long hospital stays, doctors' bills and funeral expenses come to a lot of money. We've got nothing left.'

She held his hands. 'At least we own the house,' she said. 'We don't have a mortgage hanging over our heads.'

'Yes.'

'I want to stay here, Jack. The neighbours have been so nice since…'

'Yes,' said Jack, 'I want to stay here too. I'll get a job.'

He took a deep breath and looked out of the window. He could see green leaves from the neighbouring trees, and birds wheeling in the sky. 'I want to plant a tree where the old dead one was. I'll make a little plaque saying that it's dedicated to the memory of our daughter.'

'Yes,' said Sarah.

As they lay in bed that night, she turned to him and said, 'You once said that you didn't want any more children. Do you still think that?'

'No,' he said. 'Now I know what rewards you get, however hard it is, I'd like it if we did have children. But I can't forget Gail.'

'We'll never forget Gail,' said Sarah.

The next weekend, he dug a hole and filled it with good soil before planting a young tree where the old one had been. He stood and contemplated his finished work. The new tree looked healthy and full of promise.

'Just like Gail was,' he thought. 'I'll never see her any more but the tree will always remind me of her.'

And as he stood, a large raven sat on the fence and watched him. It had no way of knowing, of course, that its descendants would one day perch in the mature tree, often to be frightened away by the children playing nearby.

As to whether it was the same bird that had caused the accident on the swing, that is impossible to tell.

Norman's Ark

'Hopeless!' he moaned. 'Absolutely bloody hopeless.' He shook his head in disbelief, the corners of his mouth turned down.

His faithful dog, a brown and white kelpie, looked up at him as though it had heard this sort of thing before.

'Bloody eejits,' he said, his latent Irishness coming out. 'And on both sides, dammit!'

The dog settled down near him. It wasn't alarmed or worried in any way.

The dog remembered when it had all started. The woman, Stella, had died. And the man, Norman, had decided that the property was just too much for him, especially since his two sons had married and moved out anyway. They weren't interested in it now, and Norman was left alone for the first time in his life; and that was why he had taken to talking to the dog.

The dog remembered when the property was split up. Men in white shirts tramping all over the place, taking measurements, making calculations, giving advice, nodding heads and shaking hands.

And so it was split into three. Norman kept the central part, on higher ground, and to the west and east of him there were created the smaller farms: still big enough to make a good living if you knew what to do.

But that was the trouble. Norman had thought that the people who bought the eastern farm seemed okay: maybe too effusive and eager, but there was no law against that, was there? So when lots of cars started turning up one Sunday morning, he was naturally curious. He went as close as he could and heard chanting and singing. Then a lone voice informed them that they were all sinners but that the Lord would save them if only they repented, and cries of 'Hallelujah' and 'Praise the Lord!'

'Hell's bell's,' he said. 'Bloody holy rollers.'

But they kept to themselves and he was grateful for that.

The people on the other side were different. He'd sold it to a young couple who said they wanted to start out on the rural life. But it soon became obvious what they meant: the rural life for them involved growing marijuana and then sitting around smoking it all day.

'Hopeless,' he said again, 'Bloody hopeless.'

He did his work, did his chores, but curiosity caused him to be mending his fence near the boundary with the holy rollers one Sunday. He heard the preacher say, 'The Lord sent a flood to cleanse the earth,' before he moved away, muttering to himself, 'Yeah! And if you religio's knew anything about the bush, you'd know that it's going to rain buckets soon. That's if you ever knew how to read the signs.'

And that's exactly what happened! The dog knew it even before Norman, of course, and made its bed in the barn just a little more comfortable. This was going to be a big one, the dog could tell.

And the rain came. And came! And came! And continued to come. Norman went out to try and save his sheep, and of course the dog went with him. They herded the sheep onto the highest spot and then there was nothing more they could do but hope that the waters didn't rise any higher.

That evening, there was a thumping on the door. There stood the holy rollers, about six of them. 'We've been flooded out,' they said. 'Can we sleep in your barn please? We've got nowhere else to go.'

'Yes. There's plenty of straw in there,' said Norman, 'It'll keep you warm. I'll get some blankets and rustle up some food for you.'

The dog wagged its tail when the people came in. It had been a long time since it had met anyone new. They made a fuss of it and settled down as best they could in the straw. One of the women came to help Norman make the soup, and for the first time in ages he found himself talking to someone other than the dog.

The soup bubbled up and was ready to serve when suddenly the door burst open and there stood the two hippies from the western farm.

'Don't you ever knock?' said Norman.

'Sorry, man, but we're washed out. Our crops have been ruined. The house's under water. We need your help, man.'

Norman turned to the woman. 'We'd better make some more soup.'

Meanwhile in the barn, the dog was having the time of its life. Everyone loved it, everyone wanted to pet it, everyone told it that it was the most gorgeous animal they had ever seen. It didn't know who to sleep with, so it moved from one to the other as the night progressed.

The next morning, it was still raining and the dog snuggled down next to the girl hippy. Norman came in with tea and eggs and bacon for them all. The dog looked up from its cosy position and wagged its tail.

And although he put a stern face on it, Norman had to admit to himself that he was enjoying all this. He stayed in the house, but he visited the barn regularly, bringing drink and sandwiches. The woman helped him and told him her name was Olive.

And so they sat in the barn, the religious group and the two hippies, the rain still falling on the tin roof, and the promiscuous dog now snuggled up to another of the religious group.

The pastor, a man called Eric, thought of organising a Bible study session but decided against it in deference to the other two guests. They, for their part, had brought a couple of reefers along but declined to smoke them, not wanting to offend their religious companions.

'There'll be lots of work to do when this is all over,' said Eric. 'We're going to have to rebuild our church.'

'Yeah,' said the hippies. 'We'll have to plant a new crop.'

Eric turned to the hippies and said, 'We'll need all the help we can get. Any chance of you giving us a hand?'

'Sure thing, dude,' said the man. 'What's in it for us?'

But his woman nudged him and said, 'We'll help you for nothing, mate. We've got to work together in times like this.'

'Thank you,' said Eric. 'And in due time we'll come and help you on your farm. Although you must realise we don't really approve of the stuff you're growing there.'

'It's not the only crop we grow,' said the man defensively. 'We grow lots of vegetables too. We're trying to be self-sufficient.'

Eric sat on a heap of straw, leaned back, and put his hands behind his head. 'That all sounds very well in theory,' he said, 'and I can see the attraction of it. But there's more to life than just growing food and then eating it. Do you do anything intellectual or spiritual?'

The hippy man's name was Ross. 'We read poetry and try to make music for each other. And when we smoke the marijuana,' he said, 'we find that to be a spiritual experience. We feel at one with the world, we see the beauty in everything, we find peace.'

Eric smiled. *I like this man*, he thought. 'It sounds a lot like prayer,' he said, 'or at least, what we try to achieve through prayer.'

'You must try it some time,' said Ross.

'I'm not so sure about that,' smiled Eric, as the dog came and laid its head on his knee. He scratched the dog behind the ears. 'I love dogs,' he said.

'I love all animals,' said Ross the hippy. 'That's why we're vegetarians.'

'Yes, we only eat meat very sparingly ourselves.'

And the dog, who was the biggest meat eater of them all, settled down with Eric. Its alliances changed and no one minded. It was everybody's friend.

After a while, all the usual remarks and platitudes of conversation had been used up.

The dog was asleep. It knew that the rain would last for the rest of the day and then stop.

Not much later, Norman, the human who owned the farm, was able to tell from the signs that the flood would soon be over. Then the real work would begin.

Even before it was light the next morning, the dog was out and sniffing the air. The rain had stopped and the dog knew that already the flood waters were receding.

Eric and Ross, the two leaders, looked at each other. 'Let's get out there and see what we can salvage,' they said.

Everywhere was sodden, of course. They squelched through the mud to the small church that the group had built and saw that the roof had collapsed. The dog ran ahead and sniffed in delight. There was a smell of rot and decay. The dog found the carcass of a dead rabbit and rolled in it. Both men laughed.

'I think this church is beyond repair, mate,' said Ross. 'Best to tear it down and start again.'

Eric the pastor stood with his hands in his pockets. 'You're right,' he said. Then he sighed. 'It took a lot of work to build it. Sunburn and blisters, and working day and night. And all lost.'

'No!' said Ross, with a vehemence that surprised even him. 'Not all lost! Come on, man! Think of the spirit of cooperation you had between you. Think of the experience gained, the friendships strengthened, the faith you had. You can't lose that sort of thing.'

Eric laughed. 'You're right, my friend.' He smiled. 'You should come and give us a sermon sometime.'

'Well, before all that, we've got to tear this down and start again. We'll start early tomorrow, eh, once it's dried out a bit?'

The pastor shook his head. 'Tomorrow's Sunday,' he said. 'We'll be having our service. All this can wait for one day.'

'Where are you going to conduct your service?'

'We'll ask Norman if we can have it in the barn,' said Eric. 'And you're invited, of course.'

'I don't think we'll have much choice,' laughed the hippy. 'Our house will still be under water.'

Ross's wife – or more accurately his partner – was called Skye. She came to meet them as they returned to the barn. 'Our house is a total disaster,' she said. She turned to Eric in explanation. 'It was a mud brick house. The flood has washed it all away.'

'Look on the bright side,' grinned Ross, 'We'll have plenty of mud to build a new one.'

The dog trudged happily into the house that Norman owned. It hadn't had such fun in years. But it looked up in alarm when it heard a yelp of disapproval, and saw the woman – Olive – standing.

'You're paddling mud through the house!'

'Don't worry,' said Norman. 'I can clean it up.'

'But what a mess!' she said.

'He's my dog,' said Norman, and that quieted her.

The dog meanwhile had sensed the atmosphere and returned to the barn, where Eric was addressing his flock.

'Tomorrow we'll hold our service in here,' he was saying, 'Then on Monday we get to work. Our new friends from the western farm will help us. And then we'll help them with their rebuilding.' He started to grow slightly pompous. 'It will be a great lesson for all of us in the power of mutual effort. Ross and Skye, of course, do not belong to our congregation but they are the children of God just like us. We need their help and they need ours. We will be rebuilding our own worlds. But with cooperation and tolerance, we will learn to become good neighbours: nay, good friends.'

Someone spoke up. 'What about this guy Norman? Will he help us? Will he let Ross and Skye through his land all the time?'

Eric smiled. 'I think Olive is helping in that regard,' he said. He may have been a religious leader, but he still knew the ways of the world. As he should.

But all was not well between Norman and Olive.

'How can you let an animal through your house like that, paddling mud everywhere?' she said.

'A house is for living in,' said Norman. 'It's not a shrine to cleanliness or neatness.'

'But for goodness' sake –'

'If all you're worried about is comfort and cleanliness in a house,' he continued, 'you're missing the whole point.'

She looked at him. 'The whole point?'

'Yes, the whole point. A house is a shelter. It's a refuge to come home to after a day's work. It's not a thing you should make yourself a slave to.'

She was quiet but obviously not convinced.

'Don't make yourself a slave to cleanliness and comfort,' he continued. 'Sure, you've got to be reasonably clean and it's good to be reasonably comfortable, but people who make that a top priority in life are not living properly.'

'You're sounding worse than Eric.'

'Eric?'

'The pastor. He's good at sermons –'

'So he should be!'

'Yeah, that's his job. But it gets you down occasionally. Sometimes I get a bit tired of it all.'

He raised his eyebrows. 'I'm surprised to hear you say that,' he said. 'I thought you were all supposed to be living together in harmony.'

'Hmmph! Well, there are cracks in the harmony.'

'That's nothing to be surprised about or even ashamed of. People living together are always going to have differences of opinion.'

'You sound like a cynical married man.'

'I was married – happily – until my wife died three years ago. Yeah, we were happy, but we still had different ideas on some things.'

'What did you do?'

'We sat down and discussed 'em,' he said. 'We usually managed to work things out, come to a compromise.'

She snorted. 'Compromise!' She said it as though it was a swear word.

'You can't be too rigid in a relationship,' said this farmer.

And again she said nothing.

The dog came in again, as muddy and as happy as ever, and the woman tightened her lips and breathed through her nose.

Norman had given permission for them to hold their meeting in the barn, but had politely declined the invitation to attend. 'I'll make you all some sandwiches and drinks for after,' he said.

But when Sunday morning came, it was threatening rain again.

'This is not looking good,' said Ross the hippy.

'No,' agreed Eric the pastor. 'I was hoping it had all gone away.'

'You gonna pray for clear skies for tomorrow?' asked Ross.

Eric smiled wryly. 'It doesn't work like that,' he said. 'You don't petition God asking for favours.'

'What do you do with your prayers, then?'

'We ask for the strength to bear whatever circumstances we find ourselves in.'

'Yeah, well, good luck. Let's hope the circumstances tomorrow are dry, eh?'

And they were. Although it was obvious it had rained overnight, the morning was bright with a chill wind.

'I'd love to help you all,' said Norman, 'but I have to attend to the sheep. They'll be pretty distressed and this cold wind won't help them.'

Everyone trudged over to the site of the church and then stood around.

'We need to fix up our living quarters first,' said Eric. 'We can't stay at Norman's for ever.'

And so the work began. Eric may have been a good preacher but he wasn't much of a handyman.

Ross, the hippy, could see what was needed and gradually became the de facto supervisor. 'Once the roads are clear again,' he said, 'we'll get into town and buy some materials.'

The other members started clearing the debris and piling it up ready to be taken away. Olive, the woman who had been helping Norman, did her best but she found herself getting in the way of the others, dropping things and tripping over.

After she had bruised her shin against some wood, Eric said, 'Maybe you can make us all a drink, Olive, and prepare some sandwiches.'

Olive wasn't so naïve as not to realise that this was his gentle way of telling her to keep out of the way. The others breathed a small sigh of relief: perhaps now they could get on with things a bit quicker.

The dog paddled around, sniffing at everything, its tail never resting from wagging, and eventually came back to the barn, where Norman had brought in a couple of lambs that had almost starved to death when their mother had died in the flood. Norman bedded them down and fed them. But they were weak and would need constant attention. He was worried. He would need sleep and the lambs would need feeding every two hours if they were to survive. He'd done that sort of thing before and he knew how hard it was. And he had been younger then.

'Well, we can only do our best, eh,' he said to the dog.

'Who are you talking to?' said a voice.

He turned and there in the doorway stood Olive.

'I thought you were helping at the church,' he said.

'I came back early. I wasn't much use there. What's the problem here?'

'The lambs are weak after being stranded. Their mother died. They'll need feeding every two hours through the night.'

'I can do that.'

'What?'

'I was no good with the work down at the church. I'll feed the lambs through the night. I'll catch up on sleep in the day.'

Norman looked at this woman and decided that perhaps she wasn't so bad after all. 'I'll show you what to do,' he said. And as they walked back to the house he said, 'You sure about this?'

'Yes,' she said, and looked as if she might say more. But didn't.

But as evening came, another problem arose. When the workers came back to the barn, weary and dirty and happy, the two fragile lambs showed obvious signs of distress.

Olive went to Norman in the house. 'They can't stay there,' she said. 'Everyone's milling around and making a row. The lambs are hating it.

'Right,' said the farmer, 'we'll bring them in here. They'll be better off in front of the fire anyway. Let's get some blankets for them to settle on.'

'You do that,' she said. 'I'm going back to the barn.' And she hurried back to ensure her charges were not being overwhelmed by all the activity.

Meanwhile, Eric and Ross and all the workers were noisily and happily washing, laughing, pulling off their boots and starting to prepare their evening meals. It had all the atmosphere of a group of people who have done a good day's work, and know it.

They settled down in the barn. They ate their evening meal, discussed briefly what needed to be done on the morrow, and went to sleep early and deeply, as only tired and happy people can.

Olive brought the lambs into the house, where Norman had prepared a big blanketed area in front of the fire. The dog followed her and sniffed at the two lambs, and wagged its tail. It knew, before any of the humans did, that the lambs would probably live if given the right attention.

Olive stayed up all night with the lambs. She kept the fire going, she fed them every two hours, and when the dog crept in to savour the warmth of the fire, she scratched it behind the ear.

The dog settled to sleep then. It knew that the woman, although no expert at farming or animal husbandry, would keep those little creatures alive.

When Norman came to her in the first grey light of dawn, she was still sitting on the floor with the lambs. They had defecated, as young animals will, but she had gathered it up and thrown it out. They were asleep now, and the dog was snoring obscenely in front of the fire. Norman laughed quietly and Olive smiled up at him.

'Will they be all right?' he asked.

'Yes, they will,' she said.

And as she looked up at Norman, she realised that she was going to be all right too. She had learnt more in the last few days than from all of Eric's sermons put together.

And the dog, of course, had known all of that even before it went to sleep.

The Blight That Man Was Born For

The world is a much better place now. Since the United Nations of Antarctica was formed, nearly a hundred years ago, we have lived in peace and comparative prosperity.

Oh, life can still be hard, to be sure, but we do not live in perpetual fear of what they used to call 'the other side' now, like they did before.

It must have been terrible.

The history books tell us that in the old days, before the Great Melting, nations – whole nations! – snarled at each other and sometimes even went to war.

What stupidity!

What stupidity, when, it seems, there was enough food to go around and no need for anyone to starve, if only they had organised themselves a bit better. The books say that some nations were very rich, that many people were even fat – can you imagine that? – but that some nations were so poor that people even starved to death.

What stupidity!

Well, one thing can be said for the Great Melting: not only did it change the face of the earth but it must have changed men's brains too, because we don't have such nonsense now.

Since Antarctica started to melt, much more rapidly than they thought, and the equatorial regions became simply uninhabitable, the pioneers who came here immediately decided that we could not afford any such dichotomies any longer. So the United Nations of Antarctica was born. All the previous countries that had laid claim to parts of Antarctica united under the one banner, the UNA, and we live together with no quarrels or selfish claims whatsoever.

We don't have time or energy for that anyway. This vast new country still has to be cultivated; we get floods and sometimes fire to deal with; but on the whole life is good and we can rise each morning with a sense of purpose, a sense that we are working towards developing this great new land. We have not brought many of our old animals from before, and we do not eat much meat now. The wildlife is abundant but we hunt and fish it sensibly so that it can constantly replenish itself.

Of course, we have brought our technology with us. Phones, trains, airplanes, electric vehicles – we have them all. The winds give us enough electricity to run them. We even brought our poetry along, and our books, and our music. We are not a savage people, oh no, not at all. Because although the Great Melting did happen much quicker than we thought, there was still time to salvage the important things before migrating south.

There are other places, of course. The South Island of New Zealand; Tasmania and the southernmost parts of the old Australia; parts of southern South America; even the southern tip of what was once Africa – all these have people living quite happily and healthily and peaceably. But the United Nations of Antarctica is the place to be, really. This, the UNA, is the country of the future. Everyone says so.

When the mass migrations began, over a hundred years ago, people from the old Europe and America went north. Anything to escape the unbearable heat of the tropics. And for a long time we thought that none of those people had survived. So when a plane touched down here near the great city of Fredericksport (over two hundred thousand inhabitants, would you believe!), and people just like us climbed out and said they were from northern Canada, at first we didn't believe them. Then they said that there were also big new settlements in what used to be called Siberia.

Their leader, or spokesman, a man called Jethro, together with his five companions, looked harder and more aggressive than we are used to.

'If they – and you – are such great civilisations, why have you never visited us before?' we asked.

'It's hard there, just like it is here,' said Jethro. 'The Great Melting opened up vast tracts of land in Scandinavia, northern Asia and northern Canada, but the transition from our previous lives was hard: hard beyond thinking. Millions of people died, and with that death came disease, and with that disease came more death. Only now are we beginning to feel that we have conquered those enemies and are able to come and make contact with you.'

Some of us laughed at that. The phrase 'Conquer those enemies' was so alien to us that it had to be explained to the younger ones, who hadn't yet read the histories, when nations were enemies to each other.

'And what do you call yourselves?' we asked. 'The United Nations of Canada and Siberia?'

Then it was their turn to laugh. 'No!' said Jethro. 'We don't have anything to do with them. We don't like them and they don't like us.'

'Why?' we asked in all innocence.

'We do things differently, that's all.'

'That's no reason to dislike them!' we said.

'Oh, it is,' he said. 'We think they want to take over our lands, and so we must arm ourselves to defend against them.'

'Why don't you unite, like we have done here?'

'We couldn't do that. They are too aggressive. They want our lands and our resources for their evil ends. That's why we have come here.'

'How do you mean?'

'There are many riches in Antarctica,' said Jethro. 'Oil, iron, just about every mineral that can be mined. We want to make a pact with you that you will let us have these minerals – for a price of course – so that we can defend ourselves against those savages from Siberia.'

'How do you know they're savages? Have you ever met any?'

'No, but they must be savages.'

'Why?'

'They don't live like us. They speak a different language. They must be fought against.'

Our leader, Frederick (some people call him Blind Freddie because he had lost the sight of one eye once on a hunting trip), spoke up. 'We cannot decide on these things immediately,' he said. 'We will consider over the next few days and let you know.'

'Good. I'm sure you will come to the right decision.'

'We will show you to your accommodation,' said Frederick.

But when they had gone, Frederick beckoned me to his side and spoke quietly. 'You must kill them tonight when they are asleep,' he said.

I gasped in surprise. 'Do you want to be so extreme?' I said.

'Yes.' Then he sighed and put his head between his hands. 'It will do no good in the long run, of course,' he said. 'More will come, and more, and still more. It's the price we pay for living in peace in a rich land.'

Frederick – Blind Freddie – is a very wise man, he has read all the poetry and philosophy and history.

He leaned back and closed his one good eye. A tear trickled down his cheek. 'It's starting again,' he said.

The Girl in the Brown Dress

I came to this town four years ago after my illness and I have settled in well here. My pension helps me live a comfortable enough life, I enjoy my garden, I attend the chess club and I have joined the supporters' club of the local cricket team.

There are times of sadness, of course. That is inevitable. I think my therapist has almost given up hope that I will ever fully recover. But as time goes by, I suppose that becomes less and less important. I can certainly remember everything since I came out of hospital. But even with the best of prompting my memory before then is hazy, to say the least.

I do have occasional flashes of scenes, strange scenes which lead me to think they are dreams that I'm remembering, rather than real occasions. And my therapist says that such things can be insights into what actually happened. I don't know. I'm beginning to lose faith in her.

I was fortunate that I had my wallet with me and so could quote my name and address, but it didn't help because everyone said that I'd not been there very long and they didn't know anything about me – any more than I did!

They put me in hospital but there was nothing physically wrong with me. Then they transferred me to the psychiatric centre, and at first they were optimistic. They said my memory would come back bit by bit. But it hasn't.

And I don't know if things that I see occasionally are real or part of a dream. My mind still gets hazy, which is why I don't win many chess games and why I sometimes forget where I've put things.

But this is a nice little town, the people here are kind to me and I am living as well as I can.

It's a quiet life and sometimes I feel that it is totally out of kilter to what I was used to. But such feelings are so vague and so rare that I cannot put any trust in them.

I was just about resigned to living the rest of my life like this when strange things started to happen. The first time was when the local community association had a gala day. There was a parade with bagpipers through the main street, and everybody stood and watched. They were heading for the park, where they had set up stalls and entertainment. I had thought I might stroll down later on. I watched them go by, when suddenly a girl in the parade, wearing a brown dress, waved to me.

'Hi, Ben,' she called.

I was astounded. I waved back in a desultory fashion and smiled: I like a pretty girl as much as anyone else, although I've given up on any chance of a real romance now.

But how strange! No one else seemed to have noticed. And that brown dress decorated with small yellow butterflies…what was it that entranced me so much about that? Was this another of my waking dreams? Did it really happen? I know my mind is not what it should be, and I did notice that nobody else reacted at all; but at the same time it seemed so real. And so puzzling.

Who was she? Who was this pretty girl? I couldn't recall having seen her around the town at all. I guessed she must have been in her mid-twenties. She had dark hair, a good figure and, most important of all, a kindly face. I still have enough wits to know that the face is the window to the soul, and that kindness is the most important thing about anyone.

I went down to the park then, amongst the community activities, but though I looked everywhere and for a long time, I couldn't find her.

But she had known me! She definitely knew me. How strange!

As the days went by, I tried to put it out of my head. It must have been a dream, I told myself. Even my therapist says I sometimes have trouble distinguishing fantasy from reality. And with my memory loss – they call it amnesia – I cannot be sure myself if it really happened.

But she did seem so real! And she definitely knew me! And I loved that brown dress of hers.

A couple of weeks went by and as the weather got warmer, I made a habit of watching our local cricket team. I have joined the supporters' club, as I mentioned earlier, and I enjoy watching them play.

This particular afternoon I was standing with a few others as our team played, when Patrick, one of my fellow spectators, said, 'Hey, look at that!'

We swivelled to where he was pointing, and there was a large flock of yellow butterflies sweeping across the far end of the ground. It must have been some sort of migration thing for them.

'Ben! Ben! Are you okay?' I heard the word faintly but I was in no condition to answer. The next thing I remember, Patrick was holding my head up and giving me a cool drink.

'You fainted, mate,' he said. 'Are you okay now?'

With the help of Patrick and some others, I got to my feet and slowly recovered. But I couldn't get the image of those yellow butterflies out of my head. They were the exact same sort of butterfly that had been on that girl's dress that day! I am sure of it! And this time it was no dream. The others had seen those butterflies, but for them it was just a passing curiosity. For me, it had triggered the memory of the mysterious girl who had waved to me.

My therapist tried to tell me that it was a sign that I was beginning to recover, because I was taking an interest in girls. Well, I had never really lost that instinct, even in my darkest times. I didn't argue with her but I didn't think much of it. As I said, I'm starting to lose faith in her.

The summer came on stronger and we had some beautiful weather. One warm morning, with nothing better to do, I strolled into town and headed for the little café where they serve a very nice coffee and cake. I nodded to a couple of acquaintances and was just stepping into the café when I caught a glimpse of brown and yellow. And there she was! Sitting at a quiet table in the little area just outside the café. She saw me and smiled and waved. But my momentum took me into the shop and I determined to speak to her once I had got my drink. But when I came out she had disappeared.

'Who was the girl in the brown dress?' I asked a fellow customer.

He looked at me strangely. 'Don't know, mate,' he said, and moved away to be with his friends.

Well, she couldn't be very far away, I figured, so I abandoned my drink and hurried down the street towards the town centre. Surely I would catch up with her there. Our town just has the one shopping mall, and I went in there with my eyes peeled. But the only person I saw who I knew was Patrick, who works there.

'Have you seen a girl in a brown dress in here?' I asked.

'No, Ben,' he said, 'and I've been here since we opened.'

Where had she got to? I have to admit I was getting a bit annoyed about it all. Why did she have to disappear just as she recognised and acknowledged me? I've heard of playing hard to get but this was ridiculous. And nobody else seemed to know anything about her.

I decided on a strategy. I would simply get out more. I reasoned that the more I mixed with the townsfolk, the more chance I had of seeing her again. Instead of staying home, watching daytime television and feeling sorry for myself, I made the effort to get out. I spent a lot of time in the shopping centre, or just walking the streets, and I joined the community association. I thought that they would be able to tell me who she was because she had been in that parade. But I drew a blank everywhere. No one seemed to know anything about a dark-haired, kindly faced girl who usually wore a brown dress.

Perhaps it really was all a dream, I told myself. My therapist said that it is possible to have what she called micro-sleeps, and in that time I suppose I could have a micro dream. Or an illusion, if you want to call it that. My therapist said that perhaps I was projecting onto some innocent person the image I had in my mind of the ideal girl. But if that was the case, why was she disappearing so quickly? Surely my 'ideal girl' would stick around and we would become better acquainted.

I became discouraged. The long hot days of summer drew on and autumn approached. And I had not seen her for a long time now.

The cricket season finished, my visits to the town centre became less frequent, and I even stopped going to the chess club. What was the point? I told myself. I hardly win any games and few of them even want to play with me. I stayed home more. I played computer games, I read trashy novels, I watched rubbish television. And my memory was not returning. Not the slightest bit. I started skipping my sessions with the therapist, and I got the feeling that she wasn't too concerned. I think she had given up on me and was just going through the motions.

As the autumn drew on, I stayed in bed for longer. There was nothing to get up for. But of course I still had to eat and, once a fortnight, I made the effort to get up, wash, shave, get dressed and go to the supermarket.

Patrick saw me once and said, 'Haven't seen you around lately.'

I smiled in faint acknowledgement but he persisted.

'You need to get out more, Ben. Come with me and the boys tonight to the pub, have a few drinks. It'll do you good.'

Well, why not? What the hell. So that evening saw me in the pub with Patrick and three or four other young men, whom I knew from the cricket club. I can't say it was a merry evening of singing and dancing, or that I met any nice girls there, but we did spend a pleasant time discussing everything from cars to horse racing to cricket, football and girls. In short, it was a typical male get together for a few beers; harmless enough and the sort of evening that is replicated countless times in countless bars every night.

I'm afraid the novelty of the occasion got to me. I drank too much.

When we left the pub, Patrick drove me home. 'You going to be all right now, mate?'

I nodded in thanks and made it inside and flopped on the bed. The ceiling was spinning. I felt terrible. 'Never again, never again,' I said to myself. Then, perhaps for the first time, I collapsed into total self-pity. I cried. I cried real tears. 'Why can't I be like everybody else?' I wailed. 'I just want to be normal!'

I slept then, but it was not a peaceful sleep. In my dream, I was climbing the outside of a high building, pulling myself up by little projections.

Some other people were helping me, but I was ahead of them and reached the very top. Somehow I had got up to the top of a smooth dome, like the famous one on St Paul's Cathedral in London. I sat at the top. Now I had to get down again. How was I going to get down this steep dome without falling off entirely? I sat there frightened to move.

It was then that I heard a voice, and I woke up. Thank goodness, it had only been a dream! But when I opened my eyes, there she was, still wearing her brown dress, bending over me, the girl with the kindly face.

'It will be all right, Ben,' she said. I heard it as clearly as anything. 'It will be all right.'

My head was spinning, I was still feeling nauseous; but I reached up to touch her – and she was gone!

I was in no condition to get up and follow her. I tried but fell. I stayed on my hands and knees for what seemed like whole minutes, although it was probably only a few seconds. But she was gone. Gone again!

Back in bed, I turned over and then slept soundly. I felt strangely comforted. At least she was still around. At least she still knew me. And I would resume my efforts to try and find her.

But it was no good. I did get out around the town again but there was never any sight of her; and no one else seemed to know anything about her. As the winter came on, I found it harder and harder to keep up my efforts. It was no fun walking around the cold streets day after day, hoping to catch a glimpse of this elusive woman. It was just easier to stay in bed.

A warm bed is preferable to a cold street. Many days I only got up to attend to my bodily needs, and then straight back to bed. My rooms got dirty. Why should I clean them? They would only get dirty again, and there was no one else to see them anyway. Cobwebs formed in the corners. I neglected to shave: nothing wrong with a beard anyway.

Once a week, I dragged myself down to the shops to buy food. Then straight back home, looking neither right nor left, not searching for the girl, interested in nothing.

I lay in bed, hugging the blankets around my neck, trying to sleep as much as possible, just to escape this dreary meaningless existence. The dirty dishes lay in the sink with food rancid and rotting on them. Blowflies buzzed and cockroaches crawled. Once, I heard a scrabbling sound and made the effort to open my eyes. There was a rat running across the room and disappearing through a small hole near the door. I didn't want to know. I closed my eyes, turned over and tried to sleep again.

Then one bitter evening I heard a knock on the door. I groaned. I didn't want Patrick or anyone else coming to try and cheer me up. Leave me alone! I thought.

But the knock came again and I dragged myself out to answer it. It was snowing outside but there, standing some distance away, was the girl! There she was! And still wearing that brown dress with the yellow butterflies.

'Come on, Ben,' she called, and started to walk away.

A new mood took me. This time I would not let her go! At last I had some hope! I followed her through the snow, hurrying barefoot, but my feet didn't hurt. The snow settled on my head and shoulders but I felt no cold. She was moving fast but I kept her in sight, even though the snow now was threatening to blot out everything. She glanced back at me occasionally. But she gradually got further and further away until I couldn't see her. There was a shaft of sunlight far ahead, strange after all this snow, but that was where she had gone and I strode towards it.

I entered the sunlit area and it was as though I had stepped into a different world. The light was bright and fresh, sparkling like an early spring morning. And then an incredible thing started to happen. Butterflies – yellow butterflies – started to descend on me. They covered me – they were so wonderful! – their soft touch on my face and hands entranced me, their beauty made me laugh out loud.

And then it came to me! My memory! I could remember! And I knew who the girl was.

With the yellow butterflies twirling around me, I stood and recalled the time I had met her. I even remembered her name: Tamyka. A slightly unusual name, but clean and crisp, like the girl herself. And I remembered about us, how we had met casually and both felt a mutual attraction. On impulse, we had agreed to go on a bushwalk together. We hardly knew each other but that didn't matter. We felt instinctively that we were soulmates.

When we met for the walk, I was surprised to see her wearing a brown dress with a yellow butterflies pattern.

'Wouldn't jeans have been better?' I asked.

'This is fine, I can move freely in this,' she said. It was a thin dress, coming halfway down her thighs, and not too tight. She moved well in it.

On that walk, we talked a lot, about everything, about ourselves, our ambitions, our likes and our dislikes. Everything. And I felt – and I'm sure she felt too – that we were going to love each other for ever.

Then the disaster. We were still modest with each other, so when we decided we both needed to attend a 'call of nature', we moved off the trail to separate areas. But then I heard a cry and a crash and when I came running I fell myself. There was a hidden sinkhole and she had fallen down it. I slid down and knocked my head. But there was Tamyka lying still.

She was dead!

Now I remembered! Now I remembered!

I climbed out and carried on, because that was when I had lost my memory. I guess it was a sort of denial. I was unable to tell anyone about her because I had blotted it out of my mind. She must still be on some police missing persons list somewhere. We hadn't told anyone else what we were going to do. Irresponsible, yes. Impulsive, yes. But we had been so full of life and promise and potential!

I remembered it all now, standing there in the bright sunlight with those yellow butterflies swirling around me. They threatened to cover me entirely, and I knew I must move on.

I felt clean and fresh and young and vigorous and vital. I was ready to meet Tamyka. I moved along and saw where I was.

I was on the bush trail where we had walked that time. The atmosphere was increasingly glorious. That's the only word for it: glorious!

And I knew then why she wore brown and yellow. Yellow, the colour of sunshine, laughter and joy. And brown, the colour of the earth, fertile and fruitful and full of promise.

I moved to where she was sitting on a log by the trail. I felt so happy!

I sat down next to her and looked into her kind face.

She smiled at me with her big brown eyes. 'Thank you for coming,' she said. 'I'm so glad you're here.'

The Protector

Part 1

'You can't be! You're too young!' she said.

'Apparently not,' he said. 'You're never too young for cancer. Even children get it.'

'But you're fit and healthy!'

'Not so healthy, I'm afraid. Doctor says I've got three months.'

'Three months! Oh God! Rod, we've only been married for six months.'

'Perhaps it's just as well we never started a family.'

She buried her head in his shoulder and sobbed. 'I can't believe it, I can't believe it!'

Rod was just as devastated as Simone. They spent a lot of time hugging and sitting quietly, thinking about their short time together.

Rod put his affairs in order. 'You'll get a lot of money from my life insurance,' he said. 'You'll be able to pay off the mortgage.'

'I'd sooner have a mortgage and you than no mortgage without you,' she said.

'You'll be a well-off widow.' He forced a smile onto his face. 'You'll be a good catch for someone.' And even as he said it his heart was wrenching.

'You know my philosophy of life,' he said. 'I believe in reincarnation. If it's at all possible, I'll come back to help you.'

'How can you do that? If you're born again, you'll be nearly thirty years younger than me.'

'According to some schools of thought,' he said, 'I could come back as any life form. I don't know, I'm not an expert. But if it's within my power, I'll come back and protect you from predators.'

'Predators?'

'You'll be a wealthy widow, like I said,' he said. 'There'll be predators.'

'I wish all this wasn't happening.'

'So do I!' he said.

Part 2

Humans can be stupid sometimes. Oh, they've realised that wherever there's a human settlement, there's almost certainly a rat within a hundred metres – and usually much closer. But how many of them really believe it?

We're good at keeping out of sight, because we know what will happen if they see us. They'll be putting down that glorious, delicious stuff that kills us.

We rats may be cunning but we can be weak also. We know it will kill us even as we eat it, but it's so irresistible! And that's where we are weak.

But we are strong in other areas. I know, somehow, some way, I have to help Simone. I don't know why; I just feel it's my destiny. But how can a common rat help a woman? All I can do is keep out of sight and see what happens.

Part 3

Well, it didn't take long. There I was in my hiding place and there she was, talking to this man. Now humans are stupid, as I said. She didn't realise it, even with her so-called women's intuition, but I knew straight away that he was no good. He was only interested in her money. So I knew what to do. I came out of my hole and deliberately ran over his foot.

You should have heard the scream! From him! And she wasn't far behind. But he bolted for the door and I knew she would never see him again.

But the predators didn't end there. Only two days later, there was another man calling round, and as soon as I saw him I knew, again, that she needed protection. This man was tall and handsome, but I could see that he was only interested in her body. Once he had seduced her, she would never see him again – that was obvious. It was time for me to do something: this time I nipped his ankle!

I swear he jumped three feet in the air! I bolted for my hole again and laughed in my way. And when I looked again, he was gone.

But here comes trouble! Simone was on the phone and I knew who she was talking to. It was the man who comes and puts down that delicious stuff for us to eat. Oh no! Oh no!

The next day, he arrived. He was a man of about thirty, with a brown beard, a slow smile and gentle eyes. 'I like the idea of reverence for all life,' he said. 'So I'm hoping this stuff will just encourage your rat to go away rather than die.'

I knew it wouldn't. That stuff, that beautiful, wondrous stuff, will kill us. I knew that.

I watched him as he put it down. It took all my willpower to stop myself from rushing out there and then to gobble it down. I tried to fight it; but I knew I would succumb to temptation in the end.

When the man had finished, I sat and watched them as she made him a drink. I saw how they looked into each other's eyes, and I saw how she smiled at him, and how he smiled back.

They talked for a long time – an agonisingly long time for me – before he left, and when he had gone, I saw how she kept smiling to herself, and moving dreamily about, and touching things.

Then I could resist no longer. I went to that stuff he had put down and I ate it all in one go. I knew what would happen. But I didn't care.

Somewhere, deep down, I was able to say to myself, 'I have done the job I promised to do. One life ends, another begins: better for me next time.'

Motor neurone disease (MND) is the name given to a group of diseases in which the nerve cells (neurones) controlling the muscles that enable us to move, speak, breathe and swallow undergo degeneration and die.

Motor function is controlled by the upper motor neurones in the brain that descend to the spinal cord; these neurones activate lower motor neurones. The lower motor neurones exit the spinal cord and directly activate muscles. With no nerves to activate them, muscles gradually weaken and waste. MND can affect a person's ability to walk, speak, swallow and breathe. Each day in Australia, two people die from MND.

There is no known cure and no effective treatment for MND.

The Motor Neurone Disease Association of Tasmania assists people living with Motor Neurone Disease and their carers by providing useful and informative information, assisting with equipment needs, raising the profile of MND in the community and raising funds for research into MND.